TRAIL TO BRIMSTONE

ALSO BY ROBERT VAUGHAN

The Tenderfoot

On the Oregon Trail

Cold Revenge

Iron Horse

Outlaw Justice

Western Fiction Ten Pack

Orphan Cowboy

Slaughter at Rebel Ridge

Reckoning Day

The Founders Series

The Western Adventures of Cade McCall

Faraday Series

Lucas Cain Series

Chaney Brothers Westerns

Arrow and Saber Series

The Crocketts Series

Remington Series

...and many more

TRAIL TO BRIMSTONE

ROBERT VAUGHAN

WOLFPACK
PUBLISHING
—— EST 2013 ——

Trail to Brimstone
Paperback Edition
Copyright © 2024 Robert Vaughan

Wolfpack Publishing
1707 E. Diana Street
Tampa, FL 33609

wolfpackpublishing.com

Paperback ISBN 978-1-63977-567-5
eBook ISBN 978-1-63977-566-8
LCCN 2024942424

Trail to Brimstone

CHAPTER 1

THE WIND BLOWING UP FROM THE CANYON WAS strong and dry, and it lifted clouds of dust to swirl high on the hot, rising air so the sky wasn't even blue anymore. It was red, like the fires of hell, and if the devil himself had stepped out from behind a rock to welcome Dane Calder to his domain, Dane wouldn't have been too shocked.

The tall man with ice-blue eyes took a measured drink of tepid water. He shook the canteen to gauge how much he had left. There wasn't much, but unless he missed his guess, the stagecoach to Dry Gulch would be along sometime today. All Dane had to do was wait for it.

Dane heard Akers's horse whicker and stamp his foot restlessly, and he looked over toward him. Hobbled, the animal was searching fruitlessly for a few blades of grass amid the brown, burned-out vegetation of the valley floor. The horse's ribs showed plainly, its eyes were glazed, and its mouth was sore. It had been ridden hard over the last few weeks and had received little attention or thanks for its efforts. Instead, Akers had let the horse fend for itself, finding food and water when and where it could.

By contrast, Dane's horse was sleek with muscle, well fed, well watered, and well curried. It was also dead, the result of a bullet in the heart sustained during the shootout with Akers. Akers killed Dane Calder's horse. Dane Calder killed Akers.

Though Akers's body lay tightly wrapped in tarpaulin, the excited hum of the flies attested to the fact that, in this heat, it would soon be getting pretty ripe. Akers's ripening body wasn't a pleasant thing to be packing along, but Dane couldn't leave him behind. He needed the body to collect the two-hundred-dollar reward. Akers had been a wanted man, a murderer. Dane Calder was a bounty hunter—a man who hunted men like Akers for the bounty the government paid for them, dead or alive.

Dane took his hat off and brushed his hair out of his eyes. The hair was dirty blond, lank and grained like oat, worn trail-weary long, just over his ears. With it repositioned, he put his hat, sweat-stained and well-worn, back on his head.

An approaching column of dust indicated that the stage was coming, so Dane threw Akers's body across the back of his horse, tied it down, then walked out to the edge of the road and waited.

"Hold on, here," the driver said a moment later,

when Dane stopped him. "You ain't plannin' on puttin' that body on this stage, are you?"

"I'm not leavin' it out here for the buzzards," Dane answered.

"Nobody said you had to do that. You could'a buried it, you know. Still can if you want. I'll wait for you."

"Can't do that, driver. He's worth too much for that. There's a two-hundred-dollar reward out for him and I'm takin' him in."

"But I'm carryin' passengers, mister. Including a woman and her little boy. I can't have them bein' bothered none with a putrefyin' body."

"They won't be bothered none. I'll just tie his horse on behind," Dane said.

"All right, I reckon that'll keep him somewhat downwind of us," the driver replied, rubbing his chin. "But, tyin' on a horse, that's goin' to cost you another fare, you know, same as if he was ridin'."

"Take that up with the sheriff when we get back," Dane said. "This is Vess Akers."

"Vess Akers?" the driver replied. He took his hat off and ran his hand through his hair, then leaned over the side of the seat to expectorate a large quid of tobacco. He wiped his mouth with the back of his hand. "Well, why didn't you say so in the first place? Mister, I'd be right proud to take that no-count skunk's body back into town. Go ahead, tie him on back. It ain't goin' to cost you nothin'."

Just as Dane started toward the horse, the door to the stagecoach opened and a well-dressed man stepped out. "Excuse my intrusion, sir. But did you say that was Vess Akers wrapped up in that tarpaulin?"

"Yes."

"You don't say," the man replied. The man walked toward Akers's horse. "Would it be all right if I just had a look?"

"Go ahead. I don't care," Dane said. "And I'm sure it won't bother Akers any."

"Yes, quite," the man replied, laughing. Tentatively, he pulled the tarp back and looked into Akers's face. It was pasty white and beginning to puff up a little. Also, the tarp allowed some of the odor to escape, causing the well-dressed man to put a handkerchief to his nose and turn away in revulsion.

"I've never seen Mr. Akers in person, of course. But I must say that this does look like his pictures."

"Mister, I ain't goin' to charge you none for him. But it's goin' to cost you a dollar and a half to ride into Dry Gulch," the driver called down.

"Driver, don't you worry any about this man's fare," the dandy said. "I'm a reporter for the *Saint Louis Intelligencer* and I'll pay for it." He smiled broadly, then looked back at Dane. "Yes, sir. It's well worth the price of an extra fare to be able to write the story of the man who killed Vess Akers."

Dane threw his saddle up on top of the coach, then tied Akers's horse, packing his body onto the back. When he climbed into the coach, he saw not only the newspaper reporter but two other men as well. One was a drummer, and the other was a gambler that Dane had run across a few times. There was also a very pretty woman who, Dane would guess, was in her late twenties or early thirties. She had her son with her, a boy of about nine. Dane touched the brim of his hat to her, and she almost imperceptibly, nodded at him, staring at him through cool, appraising eyes.

As always, when coming under such scrutiny from a woman, Dane was aware of his misshapen nose, flattened by being broken more than once in his many fights.

Overhead, the driver snapped his whip and the coach lurched forward. The side curtains were pulled shut but that did very little to keep out the dust. It did make the coach darker, though, so that its illumination was achieved by several crisscrossing bars of dust-laden beams of light. The effect was one of mottled light and dark throughout the stage.

"And now, sir, if you would tell me the story of your encounter with Mr. Akers?" the reporter asked, taking out a tablet and a pencil.

"He shot my horse. I shot him."

The reporter looked surprised. He cleared his throat and laughed, nervously. "Surely, sir, there is more to the story than that? Vess Akers was one of the most-wanted and most-feared men around. You can't pass it off so lightly."

"I can tell you how my friend Dane Calder would have done it," the drummer interjected.

"How would he have done it?" the boy asked.

"Why he would have called the man out. Yes, sir. Right in the middle of Main Street at high noon, with the whole town looking on.

"Mr. Hockensmith taught Dane Calder everything he knows," the boy said.

"Yes," the gambler added, with a knowing smile at Dane. "Mr. Hockensmith and Dane Calder used to ride together."

"Did you?" Dane asked, fixing the drummer with a steely glare.

"Well, uh, yes," the drummer answered, pulling his collar away from his neck with a fat finger. "Uh, that is, in the old days. Before I hung up my guns and took up a different profession."

"Mr. Hockensmith said that Dane Calder was going too far," the boy said. "He said he was afraid he was going to have to fight him, and if he did, he would have to kill him. He said he didn't want to kill him, because Dane Calder is his friend."

"I'm sure Dane Calder appreciates not getting killed by this drummer," Dane said.

Hockensmith cleared his throat. "Well, I, uh, don't really think it would have ever come to that," he said.

"Yes, well enough of the exploits of Dane Calder," the reporter said. "I, for one, have never thought for one moment that you could believe even half of the stories people tell about Dane Calder. I mean, no one could possibly be that heroic. On the other hand, you are here, and Mr. Akers's body is draped across his horse, back there. This is a real story, the kind my readers would love. Won't you share it with us?"

"I told you. He shot my horse, I shot him."

"But you tell the story in so few words."

"Mr. Woodruff," the gambler said, speaking for the first time, "if you recognized this gentleman, you would know that he truly is a man of few words."

"Well, that's just it," the reporter said. "I'm afraid I don't recognize him. Should I?"

"If you were a good reporter, doing your job as you should, you would recognize him," the gambler said. "But, since you don't, by all means, please allow me to make the introduction. Folks, I would like all of you to meet Mr. Dane Calder."

The reporter gasped and sat straight up in his seat.

"You?" he asked. "You are Dane Calder?"

"Yes."

The reporter looked over at the drummer. The drummer's hands were shaking now, and he took out a handkerchief to wipe his face.

"Mr. Hockensmith, is it true?" the boy asked. "Is this really Dane Calder? If he is, why didn't you say something?"

Hockensmith began to cough, then he waved his hand, indicating that he had something stuck in his throat and was unable to talk. He reached into his inside coat pocket for a flask of whiskey, pulled the cork, and took a long drink.

"I-I'm sorry, Mr. Calder," the reporter said. "I didn't mean to bother you. I hope you aren't angry. I mean…I was just trying to do my job, that's all. Please don't take offense."

Dane didn't answer the reporter or say anything to the embarrassed and frightened drummer. Instead, he leaned back in his seat and pulled the curtain aside with his finger to watch the passing countryside. He was aware of the others in the coach and of their reaction to him. The woman put her arm around her little boy and pulled him closer to her while the little boy examined him closely through wide, curious eyes. The reporter looked out the window while the drummer moved right up against the wall of the coach in order to put as much distance between him and the others as he possibly could. The gambler, smug with the satisfaction that he was able to make the positive identification, nevertheless kept his silence, most likely so as not to do anything that would upset Dane.

This was typical. Most people reacted in that same way when they were around Dane Calder. Though he technically represented law and order, there were very few names that could strike as much terror in the heart as that of Dane Calder. Mothers used it to ensure discipline in their children. "Dane Calder will get you if you don't behave." A variation on that theme was, "the bounty hunter will get you." Even though there were other bounty hunters, it was understood that *the* bounty hunter meant Dane Calder.

———

"ONE HUNDRED SIXTY, one hundred eighty, two hundred dollars," the sheriff said, counting out the money. He slid it across his desk to Dane. "Well, Calder, that closes the books on Vess Akers. Who are you going after next? Have you made up your mind?"

Dane took the money then walked over to look through the stack of wanted posters the sheriff had spread out on a table at the back of his office. He searched through them for a few minutes, then pulled one out, studied it for a moment, then showed it to the sheriff.

"What about this one?" he asked. "Have there been any changes I should know about Morgan Cottrell since I went after Vess Akers?"

"If you mean has anyone caught Morgan Cottrell, the answer is no. He's still out there," the sheriff replied. "And the reward is still open."

"That's a pretty good reward. Fifteen hundred dollars if I round up his whole gang," Dane said. "Fifteen hundred dollars is a lot of money.

"Yes, it is," the sheriff agreed. "It's about three years' salary for me."

"He's the one I'm going after."

"Well, I wish you good luck, Calder," the sheriff replied. "But I have to tell you that Morgan Cottrell is one slick son of a gun. You may have heard, Sheriff Noland and a posse of twenty men from up to Gold Springs had Cottrell surrounded here a month or so ago, but he got away from them. He got away clean as a whistle. He's goin' to be one tough man to hunt down."

"Yeah, I guess so," Dane said. "But if it was too easy, he'd be gone by the time I got there." He held up the money he had been paid. "Besides, by the time I buy a new horse and get a few things I need, I'm going to be broke again. I have to go after Cottrell, Sheriff. I need the money."

CHAPTER 2

THERE WASN'T MUCH TO THE LITTLE TOWN OF Thunder Ridge. It was hot, dry, and dusty, out in the middle of nowhere, and baking under the blows of the hot September sun. A black-and-white mongrel dog was asleep on the front porch of the general store, too hot and too unwilling to exert itself to notice the yellow alley cat who had found its own spot of shade ten feet away. On the other side of the porch two old veterans of the Civil War, one Yank and one Reb, were refighting the great conflict over a game of checkers. A couple of onlookers offered unwanted and unheeded advice. The only notice-able activity in the entire town was on the school grounds, where a group of Miss Hinton's students were laughing and playing during their afternoon recess.

Though no one in the town was aware of it, at that very moment a life-and-death drama was taking place inside the bank of Thunder Ridge.

Mr. Flournoy, the bank president, was standing against the wall alongside three bank patrons. All four of them had their hands raised and were looking through frightened eyes at the group of men who had come into the bank a few moments earlier wearing yellow dusters and brandishing guns.

There were five armed men, known collectively as the Morgan Cottrell Gang. Morgan was holding his gun on the bank teller, who was kneeling in front of the vault door, nervously twisting the combination dial.

"Mister, if you don't have that lock open in thirty seconds, I'm going to blow your brains all over the front of this safe," Morgan said.

"I'm—I'm tryin', Mr. Cottrell," the trembling teller replied. "But I'm so scared I keep makin' mistakes."

Morgan cocked the pistol and pressed the barrel against the teller's temple. "Yeah? Well, don't make any more, 'cause your next mistake will be your last one," he warned with a menacing growl.

Morgan Cottrell was in his middle forties, an average-size man whose most distinguishing feature was his eyes. They were coal black, and the right one tended to wander so that a person could never be sure where Morgan was looking. Though he didn't wear a beard for cosmetic reasons, Morgan shaved so infrequently that the lower half of his face was perpetually darkened with a heavy growth of whiskers.

"Tim, what's it look like outside?" Morgan asked.

Like Morgan, Tim had a very distinguishing feature. The lobe of his left ear had been shot off in a gunfight so that it appeared as if he had only half an ear on that side. He moved over to the window and pulled the green curtain aside so he could look out onto the street.

"It looks quiet," he answered.

There was a click as the vault door came unlocked.

"There now, that's more like it," Morgan said with a wide, evil grin. He pulled a sack from the pocket of his duster and handed it to the teller. "Now, fill it up."

The teller reached for the coin drawer.

"Not with them things! I want bank notes!" Morgan ordered, waving his pistol toward the drawer that was full of banded stacks of bills.

"Yes, sir," the teller replied, and with trembling hands he began scooping up the bank-note packages and dropping them into the bag.

"Hurry it up, hurry it up," Morgan demanded. "We ain't got all day."

In fact, Morgan and his men had even less time than he realized, for a moment earlier, the stableboy, coming to make a deposit for his employer, had seen them through the window. Slipping away quietly, he hurried back to the sheriff to give the alarm.

"It's Morgan Cottrell and his gang, Sheriff. I just seen 'em. They're robbin' the bank!"

Sheriff Noland pulled a rifle down from the gun rack and tossed it to the stableboy, then pulled down another one for himself.

"Get down to the general store," the sheriff said. "Tell anyone you find there to get ready. I'm goin' to get some help from the saloon."

Spurred on by the warning and moving quickly and quietly enough to avoid giving the bank robbers any sign of what they were doing, the men blocked off both escape routes out of town. They pushed wagons across the street to use as barricades, then with rifles, pistols, and shotguns, they took up their positions. Armed and ready, they stared back toward the bank, watching and waiting.

Through all this, no one thought to warn Miss Hinton and her pupils. The games of recess continued without interruption.

The front door of the bank swung open and five men dashed toward the horses that were tied at the hitching rail. All five were brandishing pistols. One man was also carrying a well-stuffed bag. Sheriff Noland raised up from his position and called out to them.

"Hold it, Morgan! You and your men ain't goin' nowhere!" he shouted, and at almost the same time he fired. His bullet missed the outlaws and punched through the glass in front of the bank. Another townsman fired a shot, and his bullet went through Tim's hat, knocking it into the dirt.

"What the hell?" Tim shouted. "Morgan, look out! It's a trap!"

"Let's go, let's go!" Morgan yelled, firing back as he ran to his horse. The other outlaws also began shooting as they started for their own mounts.

From the front porch of the Alhambra Restaurant, a citizen with food stains still on the front of his shirt appeared with a shotgun. He let go a blast, but the range was too great. His pellets peppered the outlaws without penetrating their skin. Another man with a shotgun fired, and the front window of the bank came crashing down.

Once the robbers were mounted, they started down the street at a full gallop, while two dozen armed townsmen fired at them from every possible position.

"I'm hit! Morgan, I'm hit!" Tim suddenly shouted, tumbling from his horse. A second later another robber went down, leaving only three who were still mounted.

"They got Al!"

Morgan and his gang reached the end of the street, only to find the barricade that had been erected.

"Damn! They got us blocked off! What'll we do, Morgan? Where will we go?" one of his men shouted in panic.

"This way!" Morgan answered, and leading the way, he started back through the town, riding back by Tim and Al who, moments before, had been shot from their horses.

Al, seeing them come back, thought they were coming for him. He stood up in the middle of the street, holding his right hand over the wound in his left shoulder. He started toward them as if expecting one of them to pick him up. When they didn't, he screamed at them. "Don't leave us, Deekus! Don't leave us!"

Tim was sitting in the street among piles of dirt and manure, watching the galloping riders through dazed eyes, almost as if he were a spectator at some stage event.

Morgan and his men were galloping hard when they came up on the barricade that had been erected at the other end of town. They had to pull up short. The horses, as panic-stricken now as the men, twisted around in nervous circles, anxious to run, but not sure where to go. It was all the riders could do to control them.

"They got us blocked off ever'where," one of the riders called.

"Follow me!" Morgan shouted. He veered off the street and headed straight for the schoolyard where the kids, who were by now frightened by the exploding gunshots, had gathered around Miss Hinton. The teacher was also rooted to the spot by her own terror.

"Hold your fire, men! Hold your fire. We might hit one of the kids!" Sheriff Noland shouted when he realized what Morgan was doing.

When Morgan and his men reached the other side of the schoolyard, they turned and fired right through the teacher and her kids, then galloped away. With shouts of anger and frustration, the men of the town ran through the schoolyard to the opposite side where they formed a skirmish line of shooters, firing at the cloud of dust as the riders grew smaller and smaller in the distance.

"Quit your shooting, men," Sheriff Noland finally told them. "You're just wasting ammunition now. They're well out of range."

"Sheriff, you ain't gonna just let them get away, are you?"

"No," Noland replied. "We'll go after them." He looked back toward the street and saw that three or four of the citizens of the town had shown the presence of mind to capture the two outlaws. "In the meantime, we got two of 'em."

"Yeah," one of the others said. "And they got two of us. Look back there, Sheriff."

"Oh, no," Sheriff Noland gasped when he noticed for the first time that Miss Hinton and a little girl were lying on the ground, victims of the outlaws' last fusillade. The fallen figures were surrounded by the other children who were looking down at their teacher and their friend in shocked silence.

"Hang them!" somebody suddenly called. "Come on, men, let's hang the bastards!"

"I'll get a rope!"

The crowd of angry townspeople started toward their two prisoners but were stopped when Sheriff Noland fired into the air.

"Hold it! Hold it!" he shouted.

The men stopped and looked back toward him.

"There won't be any lynching in my town," Sheriff Noland said coldly. "If you try it, I'll kill you, or you'll have to kill me."

"What are you tellin' us, Sheriff? That these outlaws ain't goin' to hang?"

Noland smiled coldly. "No, I ain't tellin' you that, boys," he replied. "They are going to hang. I promise you that. But it's goin' to be legal. Now, go back and get the saloon set up to use as a court-room. We're goin' to have their trial today. And somebody get the doctor for Miss Hinton and the little girl."

"Don't need a doctor, Sheriff," one of the men who had walked over to check on them said. "What we need is an undertaker. They're both dead."

———

THE FUNERALS WERE HELD three days later. Miss Hinton had no relatives in town, or anywhere close by, though someone thought she had a brother somewhere. That didn't matter, however, for the schoolteacher was well known and loved by every-one. As a result, the entire town turned out for her funeral, as well as for the funeral of the little girl who had been killed with her.

The crowd that gathered in Boot Hill for the funeral was said to be the largest body of people ever to gather in Thunder Ridge. However, there were already signs that the crowd that would witness the hanging of Tim Tyrell and Al Santos the next day would be even larger, for outsiders were already beginning to come in to town.

Though both Tim and Al had been wounded, neither of them was wounded seriously enough to stop or even delay the trial of the subsequent sentencing. As Sheriff Noland had promised, they were legally tried on the very day of their capture, found guilty, and sentenced to die by hanging, as soon as a proper gallows could be built.

The gallows was constructed in the middle of Front Street, and all who watched it go up agreed that it was a work of art—gruesome to be sure, but a work of art, nevertheless.

Everyone in town was aware of the impending hanging. The ominous sounds of hammering and sawing hung over them all—at the dinner table, at home, or the card table at the saloon. Though there was some morbid excitement over the upcoming event, the townspeople also shuddered a little, way down inside, as they contemplated the gruesome ceremony.

At the site of the gallows, someone had posted a sign:

ON THIS GALLOWS THE MASTER EXECUTIONER

AMON GALLSWORTHY WILL LEGALLY HANG

TWO MEMBERS OF THE MORGAN COTTRELL GANG,

NAMELY

TIM TYRELL

AND

AL SANTOS

FOR THE BRUTAL MURDER OF MISS EMMA HINTON,

SCHOOL TEACHER

AND MARY VERBLES,

A NINE-YEAR-OLD GIRL WHO WAS HER STUDENT.

ADMISSION TO THE EVENT IS FREE

Dane Calder rode by the sign slowly, sizing it and the little town up. He was wary as always when riding into someplace for the first time. He looked over the buildings, adobe for the most part, though a few were made from whipsawed lumber, their unpainted boards turning gray and splitting.

Dane rode up to the hitch rail in front of the saloon, dismounted, and patted his tan duster a few times, sending up puffs of red dust that settled back again with grim determination. He looked up and down the street, aware of a sign that was creaking in the wind and the flies buzzing loudly around a nearby pile of horse manure. Seeing no one nor anything of particular interest, he went inside the saloon.

"Welcome, friend, welcome!" the bartender said as Dane pushed his way through the batwing doors. Inside the saloon it was shaded and cool and full of people. A piano ground away at the back of the room and a half-dozen bar girls, with bare shoulders and painted faces, moved through the crowd, patting bald heads here and pushing away roaming hands.

"First drink is on the house," the bartender said. "A celebration, you might say."

"Whiskey," Dane grunted.

"Yes, sir, whiskey it is. Do you want to know what we are celebrating?" the bartender asked as he poured Dane's whiskey. Dane looked at him without replying. "Well, I'll tell you what we're celebrating," the bartender went on, even though Dane gave him no indication that he was interested. "We are celebrating a hangin'. Tomorrow morning at ten o'clock sharp, we'll be sendin' those two galoots we got down there in jail, straight to hell. Maybe you didn't know this, but they're members of Morgan Cottrell's gang. I reckon you've heard about Morgan Cottrell? Anyway, he tried to rob the bank here, but the good folks of this town gathered round and shot up his gang pretty good. Shot these two right out of the saddle, we did."

"Did you get Morgan Cottrell?" Dane asked. His voice was quiet and low-pitched, a little like the rumble of distant thunder.

"He got away," the bartender said.

"Did he get away with the money?"

"Well, yes, sir, I reckon he did."

"Then what do you have to celebrate?" Dane asked, taking the drink and turning his back to the bar to look over the room.

Another customer came in a moment later, then moved down the bar to stand right next to Dane. He pushed Dane aside.

"You're crowdin' me, mister," he said.

Obligingly, Dane moved.

The man moved with him and pushed his again.

"You're still crowdin' me."

Dane moved again, and so did the man.

"You're still crowdin' me," the man said a third time. He pushed Dane away again.

Dane looked at the man coldly. "I don't know what you got stuck in your craw, mister, but I'm not moving again," Dane said.

Suddenly, and unexpectedly, the stranger tossed his drink into Dane's face.

Dane's response was just as unexpected. Because he wasn't actually facing his adversary, everyone including the man who had tossed the drink thought he would have to turn before he could respond. Instead, Dane slammed his elbow into the man's chest with such force that the man dropped his glass and grabbed his chest with both hands. When he did, Dane hit him in the nose with a hard left, then finished it up with a short but extremely powerful right to the chin. The man dropped to the floor.

"Who was this—" Dane started to say, but that was as far as he got before the lights went out. Someone from behind had hit him over the head.

CHAPTER 3

MORGAN COTTRELL SLAMMED THE DOOR SHUT behind him and walked outside to check on the horses and to relieve himself. He and his gang had spent the night at a small spread they had run into where a man, his wife, and daughter lived.

A faint streak of gray light in the east had told Morgan that it was nearly dawn. Before leaving the house, a few moments earlier he had ordered the woman to start breakfast.

When he returned to the kitchen it was filled with the rich aroma of coffee. Bacon was sizzling in the pan and the daughter had just taken a pan of biscuits out of the oven.

"Did you see anything out there?" Gus asked, as he grabbed a hot biscuit.

"Nothin' I wasn't supposed to," Morgan answered.

"I sure hope ever'thing went all right with Parish."

Morgan chuckled. "What could go wrong? All he had to do was get hisself throw'd in jail."

Gus laughed. "Yeah, I guess you're right."

"Give me some bacon and let's get outta here," Morgan said.

"Do we have to leave so soon?" Gus asked as he sidled up to the young girl.

"Leave my daughter alone," the man said as he moved toward Gus.

"Hold on there, mister. Gus ain't done nothin'," Morgan said as he pulled his gun and shot the man before he could get to Gus.

"Manny," the woman cried as she kneeled at her husband's side. "Why did you do this? We let you spend the night in our home and we are feeding you breakfast."

"That's so," Morgan said. "And since you was so nice to us, I'll let you stay with your husband, and you, too, honey." With the gun still in his hand he fired two shots.

"Take the rest of them biscuits, and let's go," Morgan said without even looking at the three people he had just killed.

———

"TRY IT AGAIN!"

The shouted instructions were followed by a heavy bump, then the sound of a trapdoor swung open.

"Yeah, that's it. It's ready to go now. Let's go over to the Alhambra and get us some breakfast."

The shouts back and forth and the sound of the mechanism being worked floated in through the open bars of the jail, awakening Dane Calder.

Dane opened his eyes, tipped his hat back, and looked through the bars that separated his cell from the cell next to his. There were two men in that cell, and while one was lying on his bunk, the other was standing on a stool near the back window, looking through the bars.

"I can see it, Tim," the man at the window moaned. "Oh, damn, there it is! Look at it."

"Now, Al, what the hell do I want to look at it for?" Tim asked. "When it comes time for us to make that last walk, I reckon I'll be seein' it close enough."

"What do they want to hang us for?" Al asked. "We didn't shoot that schoolmarm and the little girl. Hell, we was both layin' in the street, near to death when that happened."

"I wouldn't call a nick in the shoulder and a couple of pellets in the leg near to death," Tim said. "Hell, you can't hardly even see the wounds now."

"Well, that don't matter. We didn't shoot that schoolteacher and kid, and it ain't right that we gotta hang for it."

"You heard what the judge said," Tim explained. "We was in the act of committin' a—a *felonious crime*," Tim said, stumbling over the words, "when innocent civilians got theirselves kilt. That makes it first-degree murder, whether we done it or not."

Dane, who was wide awake now, sat up on his bunk and, feeling a soreness on top of his head, rubbed it gingerly. There was a very painful bump there, and he could feel that the bump was surrounded by a dry crust of blood. He had been hit on the head, hard, the night before. For a moment, he was confused as to why, then it all came back.

Someone in the bar had picked a fight with him. There had been no reason for it. Dane was minding his own business, standing at the bar having a drink, when the man next to him began goading him. As he recalled, Dane had shown what he figured was an amazing degree of tolerance before he ended it. That was the last thing he remembered until he woke up a few moments ago and saw that he was in jail.

Dane looked around the jail to take stock of his situation. The jail was housed in a brick building, with two cells at the rear and the sheriff's office in front. Dane was in one of the cells; the two condemned prisoners were in the other. The question was, where was the fellow who had picked the fight with him? If Dane was in jail, he should be too.

Dane knew who the other two men were. Dane knew, not only because of what he'd learned yesterday, but because he had been trailing Morgan Cottrell and his entire gang for nearly six weeks. He didn't just happen to ride into Thunder Ridge yesterday; he was there because Morgan Cottrell's trail had led him there.

Dane was a bounty hunter who operated on the right side of the law, though outside the boundaries that constrained more traditional lawmen. As a bounty hunter who specialized in "dead or alive" quarry, Dane searched out and captured, or destroyed, the very dregs of society—those outlaws whose evil behavior had marked them as do heinous that the courts wanted their activities terminated. Morgan Cottrell, who was wanted dead or alive, was one such man. There was a one-thousand-dollar reward for Morgan Cottrell's carcass, and a lesser amount for each of his men. That was all the incentive Dane needed to go after him.

Dane got up from his bunk, stretched, and walked over to look, silently, through the barred windows at the back of his own cell. From here he could see the view that had so unnerved Al. He grunted, then turned away.

"Have they served breakfast yet?" he called over to Al in the next cell.

Al looked at Dane with an expression of hate and anger. The anger was that Dane could be so obviously insensitive to the situation as to inquire about food.

"Breakfast? Do you think I'm worried about breakfast? You're askin' about breakfast, and I'm about to be hung."

"Hell, mister, that's your problem, not mine. I'm

not about to be hanged and I'm hungry," Dane replied.

"Who the hell are you?"

"The name's Calder," Dane said. He saw a washbasin and a pitcher of water at the back of his cell and went over to wash his face.

"Calder?" Tim said from his bunk, raising up on his elbows. "Dane Calder?"

"That's right," Dane answered.

Tim tugged on his half-ear. "Would you be the one they call *the* bounty hunter?"

"I've been called that," Dane admitted, drying his face on a towel that hung from a hook beside the washbasin.

Tim laughed.

"What the hell you got to be laughin' about?" Al asked, swinging around angrily to confront his cell mate. "I don't see nothin' funny about any of this."

"Why, Al, don't you know who this here fella is?" Tim asked. "He's the man that's been doggin' us all this time...the man that's been keepin' us on the run. This here is Dane Calder, the famous bounty hunter. He catches folks like you and me for the reward money. Only there ain't nothin' he can do now, 'cause we're already caught." Tim laughed out loud. "We're gonna hang, and he ain't gonna make one cent out of it. Don't you think that's funny?"

"Damnit, Tim, you're crazy, did you know that?" Al asked. "You're crazier than hell."

The front door of the sheriff's office opened then, and the sheriff came in from the street, leading the man who had picked the fight with Dane in the saloon the night before. Both of the man's eyes were black and his nose was badly swollen from his encounter with Dane. So, he didn't go free after all.

"Mister, I don't understand you," the sheriff was saying to the man as they came in. "The judge just offered to let you work off your fine by cleaning up the saloon, and you told him you'd rather have thirty days in jail."

"I don't do no work unless I get paid for it," the prisoner answered.

"Yeah? Well, you might have spent last night in the doctor's office, but you won't be spending any more nights there. You're in my jail, now, and you're going to be here for a month. And don't think I'm going to let you just lie around on your backside for the next thirty days, either. No, sir, you're going to earn your way." The sheriff shoved him toward Dane's cell.

"You're Dane Calder, aren't you?" the sheriff asked.

"Yes."

"Thought I recognized you. How's your head?"

Dane put his hand to the bump. "It hurts," he replied. "Who hit me?"

"My deputy. He was over at the saloon when the fight started."

"Then he knows it wasn't my fault."

"Yeah, he told me. But he was afraid you was gettin' ready to kill this fella, and if you had, that would have made things a lot more complicated.

You damn near killed him as it is. You hit him in the chest as hard as if he had been kicked by a mule, and the doctor was afraid you might of done some real damage to his innards. By the way, I don't reckon anyone made any proper introductions between you and this gent last night. His name is Parish. You chasin' after him?"

"Never heard of him," Dane replied. "Parish, you mind tellin' me what we were fightin' about?"

"I was drunk," Parish muttered. "Sheriff, you ain't going to put me in there with him, are you?"

"Well, I reckon I am."

"No, that ain't right. I'm afraid to get in the same cell with him right now."

"Can't say as I much blame you," the sheriff answered. "But I gotta put you in there, Parish. It's either go in with him, or else you get put in with Tim and Al, here. Of course, seein' as they're gonna be hung in a couple of hours, you'd have the cell all to yourself. I guess I could put you in there with them, if that's the way you want it."

"That's the way I want it."

"All right," the sheriff said, sighing. He unlocked the door to Tim and Al's cell and shoved Parish inside with them. "You fellas got company," he said.

"What about me, Sheriff?" Dane asked. "Seeing as your deputy can testify for me, when do I get to see the judge?"

"Prob'ly not until this afternoon," Sheriff Noland replied. "We got this hangin' to get took care of before the judge will hear any more cases.

You hungry? Want some scrambled eggs and coffee?"

"Yeah, that'd do good right now," Dane said.

"Got some out here on the stove," the sheriff replied. "I'll get some for you."

The sheriff handed Dane a tin plate of scrambled eggs and a cup of coffee, then offered the same thing to the other prisoners, who declined. He was just returning to the front office when the door opened and another man came in. The new arrival was wearing a long, dark-colored frock coat, and a high-crowned, stovepipe hat. Dane recognized him as Martin Galsworthy, the professional hangman.

Martin walked up to the bars of Tim and Al's cell. He lifted his high hat just an inch, as a way of greeting.

"Good morning, gentlemen," he said. "How are we feeling this morning?"

"Now, how the hell would *you* feel on the day of your hangin'?" Al replied.

"Oh, a little queasy, I guess," Martin said. "But then, I always do feel that way when I'm about to send somebody off to perdition." He took out a tablet and pencil and studied the two condemned men with such intensity that Al's nerves broke.

"What are you lookin' at?"

"I'm just trying to do a good job, that's all," Galsworthy replied. "After all, you fellas aren't goin' to be lynched, you're gonna be executed, dignified and proper. Now you," he said, pointing to Al, "how much do you weigh?"

"I don't know. 'Bout a hundred fifty pounds or so, I reckon," Al said.

"And you?" He pointed to Tim.

"A hundred seventy, maybe a hundred eighty pounds," Tim answered.

Galsworthy made the entries in his book, then he folded his book shut and put it in his pocket. He smiled at the prisoners.

"Got everything I need now to make this a nice, dignified hangin'. No danger of anyone chokin' to death or havin' his head pop off when the knot snaps the neck."

Involuntarily, Al shivered.

"I have to go now," Galsworthy went on. "There are several folks outside wanting me to autograph the souvenir program of the hangin'. I don't think I ought to disappoint 'em." He looked over toward Dane's cell as he started out, then he stopped.

"Have mercy, you're Dane Calder, aren't you?"

"Yes."

Galsworthy smiled. "Mister, you've cost me a lot of business, did you know that?" he asked.

"How?"

"When you go after a man, more often than not, you bring home a putrefying carcass and collect your reward. That doesn't leave much for me, I'm afraid." He chuckled. "Though it wouldn't surprise me greatly, Mr. Calder, if I didn't come into some little town somewhere, someday, and find out that *you* were my subject."

"You never can tell," Dane said.

"Don't worry though," Galsworthy went on. "If I ever do have to hang you, I'll give you my finest service. It'll be quick and easy."

"That's kind of you. And if I ever have to shoot you, I'll show you the same courtesy," Dane replied.

Galsworthy cleared his throat nervously. "Uh, yes, to be sure." Then, clearly anxious to be gone, he looked over at Noland. "Sheriff, would you mind stepping out to the gallows with me for a bit? I have a few last-minute details I want to go over."

"Yes, of course," Sheriff Noland answered. He looked at the two condemned men. "If you fellas are wantin' a few minutes to make peace with your Maker, better take 'em now," he said. "When I come back, I'll be takin' you out of the cell for your hangin'."

"We ain't gonna hang, Sheriff!" Al called. He rushed over to grab the bars of his cell and yelled at Sheriff Noland, who was just starting out the front door. "We ain't gonna hang, do you hear me?"

"Al," Tim hissed. "Take it easy."

As Dane continued to eat his breakfast, he studied the three men in the other cell.

"What are you starin' at?" Al called over to Dane. "How can you sit there, eatin' breakfast like that, knowin' we're about to be hung?"

"I'm hungry," Dane replied. "Besides, like I told you, I'm not the one that's about to hang."

"Yeah? Well, maybe we ain't either," Al said.

CHAPTER 4

BY TEN O'CLOCK, SEVERAL HUNDRED PEOPLE HAD gathered in town for the hanging, and more were coming. Wagons were rolling in carrying whole families and picnic lunches. All manner of men were present, some in suits and some in cowboy garb. There were women too, the painted variety, "soiled doves" from the saloon and bawdy houses, as well as proper women, wives and mothers in long dresses and sunbonnets. Children ran through the crowd, excited by the prospect of actually seeing a double hanging. The pupils from Miss Hinton's school had been given a special place of honor right down in front.

Vendors worked the crowd, selling lemonade, beer, pretzels, popcorn, and sweet rolls. The town looked as if it were celebrating the Fourth of July, and indeed, the gallows had been decorated with red, white, and blue bunting, even though a few had commented that such colorful bunting seemed in particularly poor taste.

A black-frocked preacher climbed up on the gallows and stepped out to the edge, using that opportunity to deliver a sermon. Twin nooses hung from the crossbeam that ran across the top of the gallows, and the preacher pointed to them as he spoke in a loud, oratorical voice.

"My friends," he said, "today we are gathered here to watch two of God's children be hurled into eternity. We are sending them to meet their maker with blood on their hands and sin in their hearts."

"And good enough for them too, Preacher!" someone shouted from the crowd. Some cheered, and many laughed, but the preacher held out his hands to call for quiet.

"I was over to the jailhouse this mornin', and I asked both of 'em to get down on their knees with me…to get down on their knees and pray to the Lord for forgiveness." He was silent for a moment. "But they didn't do it, friends. Neither one of 'em repented of their sins. You know what that means, don't you, friends?"

"They're goin' to hell," someone shouted, and again there was laughter and cheering.

"You are right. Them two souls is lost, doomed forever to the fiery furnaces of perdition…doomed to writhe in agony forever!"

The preacher literally shouted the last few words, and so graphic was his delivery that a few of those close to him shivered involuntarily at his powerful imagery. They looked up toward the gallows, and one or two of them touched their necks fearfully. A few souls even managed to sneak a drink from a bottle.

"It's too late for them. It's too late, I say," the preacher continued. "But it's not too late for you, my friends. Repent! Repent now, I say, for the wages of sin are death and eternal damnation!"

The preacher's voice carried well and was heard easily by the four men who were back in the jail.

"Lister to that holy-roller, will you?" Tim said. He chuckled. "He's preachin' hisself a sermon, ain't he?"

"You sound like you're enjoyin' it," Al said.

"Yeah," Tim said. "It reminds me of bein' back home in Missouri. The whole family used to go out to an all-day preachin'. The ol' man would listen to it, get religion, then when we got back home he'd beat the hell out of ma and us kids, because of all the sinnin' we had been doin'. Then one day I decided I didn't want to take it no more, so I just picked up the shotgun and blowed his damned head off." He giggled, almost insanely.

Parish had been standing on the bed looking out the back window during Tim's story. Now he came back and called the other two around him. They exchanged a few whispers, speaking so quietly that Dane couldn't hear what they were saying. That didn't bother him; he had no desire to hear what they were saying.

Every few minutes after that, one of the three of them would walk back to the window and check the gallows. Dane found that a little strange. If he were about to be hanged, he certainly wouldn't be interested in studying, so closely, the instrument that was going to do the job.

Dane was just taking the last swallow of his coffee when Parish climbed up on the stool for another look. When he came back this time, he shook his head yes, then said something in a low, quiet voice. Nodding, Tim and Al picked up the thin, straw-stuffed mattresses from their bunks, then all three of the men got down on the floor in the corner of the cell that was farthest from the rear wall. They pulled the mattresses over them.

"What the hell?" Dane asked, looking at them, puzzled by their odd behavior. Then suddenly he realized what must be going on, and he dived for the floor in his own cell just as an explosion went off. A large deafening blast of dynamite took out the entire back wall, letting in daylight not only to the condemned prisoners' cell but to Dane's as well.

"Good job, Parish!" someone shouted from outside the jail.

Dane sat up and began brushing the pulverized brick dust away from him. He stared through the large, billowing cloud of smoke and dust and saw Morgan Cottrell and another mounted man. In addition to their own horses, they were holding the reins to three others.

Parish, Tim, and Al scrambled across the rubble to grab the horses that were being held for them.

"I got to hand it to you, Morgan. Your idea of me pickin' a fight to get thrown in jail was a good one," Parish said. He rubbed his chin. "Only next time, I'll be a little smarter about who I pick it with."

Now the mystery of last night's disturbance made sense to Dane. Though Parish wasn't someone Dane knew, he was obviously a part of Morgan Cottrell's gang. Parish had gotten himself thrown in jail so he could help coordinate the jailbreak. That also explained why Parish turned down the judge's offer to work off the fine.

Even as Dane was contemplating this, Parish mounted his horse and almost casually tossed another lighted stick of dynamite into the pile of rubble that had been left by the first explosion.

"Sorry, Calder, but we don't need to leave no witnesses!" Parish shouted.

"Let's get out of here!" Morgan called.

Dane's first thought was to chase after them, then he heard the sizzle of the fuse on the stick of dynamite Parish had just tossed, so he dived for cover. An instant later the second stick went off, and this blast brought down the rest of the jailhouse.

Dane protected himself from the blast as best he could. Though he could find no proper cover, he did manage to shield his head by covering it with his folded arms. Despite that, his body was pretty well pummeled by falling rocks and bits of brick.

When the dust and smoke settled from the

second explosion, Dane stood up, realized that he wasn't badly hurt, and stepped out into the alley, or rather, what had been the alley. It was now so full of rubble it was completely blocked off. He became aware at that moment, of the screams and shouts of excitement coming from the crowd that had gathered for the hanging.

"What the hell was that?" someone called.

"It sounded like an explosion," someone answered. "Only there was two of 'em."

"It came from the jail!"

Having located the blast, the townspeople began moving to the scene, running hard toward the still-smoking pile of rubble that had been the jail. The sheriff and the hangman were among the first on the scene. When the sheriff arrived, he saw Dane standing in the alley, covered from head to toe with pulverized brick dust. Angrily, the sheriff pointed his pistol toward Dane.

"Don't move, mister. You ain't goin' nowhere! Get your hands up!" he shouted. A half-dozen other armed men also aimed their guns at Dane.

Slowly, so as not to frighten them into doing anything foolish, Dane raised his hands.

"Sheriff, I'm afraid you're a little late," Dane said. "They're gone."

"What happened here?"

"Turns out that Parish was one of Morgan Cottrell's men. Cottrell just blasted all three of 'em out of here."

"Damn," Noland swore as he took off his hat

and threw it on the ground. He put his gun away. "Get your horses, men!" he shouted. "Everyone get mounted. We're goin' after them!"

"What about this fella?"

"Does he look to you like he's one of 'em?" the sheriff answered in exasperation. He picked up his hat, then turned to Dane. "Leave him be."

Following the sheriff's lead, the men put their pistols away and started after their horses. Dane was left standing alone in the alley, his hands still in the air. He looked around, then lowered his hands, and with a shrug walked across the street to the saloon. He realized that there was no sense in his going after Morgan until the others came back. They would just get in his way. Besides, unless he missed his guess, the reward would be going up.

Dane found a table in the corner of the saloon, picked up a deck of cards, and began playing solitaire. He waited.

————

THAT NIGHT, Dane was nursing a beer, having just polished off a steak that he charged to the city. "After all, I'm still a prisoner," he told the proprietor, "and the city has to feed me."

"I hear a bunch of horses outside," someone in the saloon said. "You reckon the posse's comin' back?"

"Take a look, Harvey."

One of the others in the saloon carried his beer over to the batwing doors and looked out into the street. He saw several lead-footed horses, with riders sitting tired and heavy in the saddles. "Yeah," he answered. He took a swallow of his beer, then added, "I'd say that's them, all right. They look like they been ridin' through hell."

A third man verified it a moment later when he came in the door and pushed up to the bar.

"Give me a beer, George," he said to the bartender. Then turning, he gave his report to the others in the saloon. "I was just down to what's left of the sheriff's office when the posse come in. They didn't catch nobody. But they did find Fernandez and his wife and young'un."

"What do you mean? What are you talkin' about?"

"You know Manny Fernandez. He's got a little spread just west of here. Well, the posse stopped by to see if they had seen anything and found all three of 'em dead. Shot right through the head...all of 'em."

"Morgan Cottrell do that?"

"Well, it sure wasn't Indians," the man said.

"They got to be caught. That's all there is to it, gents, them bastards got to be caught. They don't deserve to live."

"They'll never get caught now."

"Not unless somebody real good was to go after 'em. Somebody like Dane Calder."

There was a hurried exchange of harsh whispers between the bartender and the one who had just arrived. The bartender pointed to Dane. After that, the man who had mentioned his name turned and looked toward the corner table where Dane sat, nursing his beer.

"Don't mean no disrespect, Mr. Calder," the man said, holding his beer in salute, "but I meant what I said. The only way Morgan Cottrell and them fellas with him is ever gonna be caught is if someone like you was to get on their trail."

Sheriff Noland came in through the front door just as the man made his announcement. The sheriff looked at Dane for a moment, then brushed the trail dust off his clothes with his hat. After that, he stepped up to the bar and ordered a large mug of beer. The bartender drew the beer, then pointed to the empty plate on Dane's table and said something, speaking so quietly that Dane couldn't hear. The sheriff chuckled then brought his beer over and sat down across the table from Dane.

"George tells me you had your supper at the expense of the town."

"Yeah. You got me in jail, remember? Feedin' me is your responsibility."

"We normally give our prisoners beans, not steak," the sheriff said.

"Well, I guess I didn't read the menu," Dane replied laconically. "I heard about the rancher and his family."

"Yeah," the sheriff said, taking a swallow of his

beer. "Only thing is, I think that was done early this mornin'. There was some cold bacon in the skillet, and a few cold biscuits on the table. I think they was just fixin' breakfast. Besides, we was chasin' 'em too hard for 'em to have time to do anything like that after they come here."

"It's probably where Cottrell spent the night while he was plannin' the jailbreak," Dane suggested.

"Yeah, that's my figurin'. Anyway, we buried them out there. Morgan Cottrell is runnin' up quite a score, if you ask me. Two women, two kids, and a man, just in the last few days. To say nothin' of what all he'd done before he come here."

"He's pure evil, all right," Dane said.

"I guess you know him and his bunch got away," the sheriff went on.

"Yeah," Dane said again. He took another swallow of his beer.

"Calder, I'd like to deputize you to—"

Dane held up his hand and shook his head.

The sheriff laughed. "I didn't think that would work," he said. "But maybe this will. I just met with the judge. The bank is offering a fifteen-hundred-dollar reward on top of what's already out. But it will only be paid after the entire gang is eliminated. The government's offerin' two hundred dollars for each of his men, and fifteen hundred for Cottrell himself. Put all that together, and you'd have fifty-three hundred. Are you interested?"

"The government money is dead or alive. What about the reward offered by the bank?"

"Dead or alive," the sheriff said.

Dane finished his drink, then got up and walked out of the room without answering. But then Dane was aware the sheriff knew that no answer was necessary.

CHAPTER 5

THE SUN WAS ALREADY LOW ON THE WESTERN horizon as Dane rode into Vista del Sol. The hollow clump of his horse's hooves echoed back from the buildings that fronted the dusty little plaza that was the center of town. Vista del Sol was a little more Mexican than Thunder Ridge, which was more American than Tierra Roja, which was more Mexican than Silver Creek. In reality, Dane had learned it didn't make any difference whether they were Mexican or American. Sometimes, as in this one, the towns were a scattering of adobe buildings laid out around a dusty plaza. Sometimes they were false-fronted buildings facing a rutted street. But always, when the curtain was pulled aside, they were the same.

It was about suppertime, and Dane could smell the spicy aroma of meals being prepared in the homes, the Mexican smells of beef, peppers, beans, and tortillas, interspersed here and there with the more American aromas of pork chops and fried chicken.

Dane dismounted in front of the livery stable, and a boy of about fifteen came toward him. The boy was Mexican, with dark hair and eyes, and skin that might have been three shades lighter if he would take a bath. He was eating a bean-filled tortilla, and the sauce was running down his chin. A cloud of gnats hung around his head.

"Take care of your horse, señor?"

Dane took his saddlebag off and draped it across his shoulder, then pulled the Winchester from its sheath. "Feed him oats. Give him a good rubdown," he ordered.

"Si, señor," the boy answered.

"I'm looking for five hombres, riding together," Dane said. "*Banditos*. Their trail leads here."

"Maybe there were some men like that yesterday," the boy said. "I do not know."

"Did they leave their horses with you?"

"No, señor. They left the horses tied in front of the cantina all night. This morning when I looked, they were gone."

"Can I get something to eat in the cantina?"

"Si, señor," the boy said. He smiled. "The tamales—muy bueno!"

"Gracias."

Dane walked across the square to the cantina. Unlike the saloon in Thunder Ridge, this place didn't have batwing doors Instead, several strings of brightly colored glass beads guarded the entrance, and they clacked loudly as he stepped through them. For a brief moment all conversation stopped as everyone looked toward him. Even the bartender noticed Dane's entrance, though he was busy lighting the lanterns on a wooden frame that had been lowered from the ceiling.

"I'll be with you in a minute," the bartender said. As if that were the signal, the others in the saloon resumed their private conversations. The Mexican influence in the town was strong enough that several of the conversations were in Spanish, though most of the patrons appeared to be American. However, there was such a jumble of words from the various conversations that Dane was unable to pick up anything.

The pulley squeaked as the bartender pulled the wooden frame back up to the ceiling, then tied off the rope. The just-lit lanterns spread their soft golden light over the inside of the cantina, pushing back the deep evening shadows that had begun to fill the corners.

"What'll it be?" the bartender asked.

"Beer, and something to eat."

"We got beef, beans, ham and eggs—" the bartender started.

"Tamales."

The bartender chuckled. "You must've boarded your horse with Garcia. His mama furnishes the tamales, so he touts them to everybody. You sure that's what you want?"

Dane glared at the bartender but said nothing.

"All right, all right. I'll bring them right out," the bartender said, unnerved by Dane's unwavering stare.

Dane found a table to his liking. He leaned his rifle against the wall, then sat down, dropping the saddlebags on the floor alongside his chair. A girl walked over to his table and smiled down at him. Her eyes flashed darkly, and she brushed her hair aside as she looked at him.

"I am Carmen," she said. "If you like, I will have a drink with you."

Dane smiled and tapped his finger on the table, indicating she could sit down.

"Tequila," she called over to the bartender. Then to Dane, she said, "You have come from far away?"

"Far enough," Dane said. The bartender brought tequila for the girl and a plate of tamales for Dane. Dane stripped off the corn husk and began eating one. "Are you here every night, Carmen?"

"Si, every night."

"I'm looking for five men who were here last night. The leader has an eye—" Dane began, but Carmen interrupted him.

"Si, *mal de ojo*," the girl said. "An evil eye."

"You might say that. You saw him then?"

"Si."

"Where did they go?"

"The man with the evil eye. He is your friend?"

"No."

Carmen put her hand across the table and let it rest lightly on his.

"Señor, when a woman is…with a man…she can tell many things about him. It is not an accident that the man you seek has the mark of Tierra Roja. He is an evil man."

"I agree, Morgan Cottrell is no saint," Dane said.

"If he is not your friend, why do you look for him?"

"The law wants him."

"You are a lawman?"

"No, I'm a bounty hunter."

"Oh, I see. Then you are a man who hunts other men for money."

"Yes."

"This is dangerous, is it not?"

"It can be," Dane agreed. "Do you know where they went?"

"No. When I woke up this morning, I heard them leaving. I watched from my window."

"Which way did they go when they left town?"

"That way," the girl said, pointing northwest. She smiled and dropped her hand from his hand to his knee. "It is too late for you to go after them now," she added. "You will have to spend the night in Vista del Sol. Would you like to spend it with me, señor?"

Dane reached down and took hold of her hand, then put it back on the table. "If I stay with you tonight, I may want to stay with you every night," he said, smiling at her. "And if I did that, I wouldn't get any work done." He fished a couple of coins from his pocket, then dropped them on the table. "But I want to thank you for your information." He got up and started for the door.

"Dane Calder," Carmen called to him as he left, "you must be very careful."

"I'll try," Dane replied.

Dane was halfway across the dark square when he suddenly realized that the girl had called him by name. *How did she know it? He hadn't told her.*

Dane turned to go back inside when he saw them. Two Mexicans jumped from the shadows and came at him with knives, which they were swinging in low, vicious arcs. It was only because of his lightning reaction that the first thrust didn't completely disembowel him.

Despite his quickness, one of the attackers did score, and his knife opened up a wound in Dane's side. Dane fell, then rolled through the dirt to get away. He had no idea how badly he was hurt, he was aware only of a searing, burning feeling, as if someone had put a hot poker against his side.

Realizing that Dane was hurt, the other attacker moved in quickly, planning to take advantage of the situation and finish Dane off.

Dane rolled over onto his back, and as the attacker rushed to him, he thrust his feet out, catching the Mexican in the groin, not only driving him back, but momentarily taking him out of the fight The other one, not yet realizing that he was alone, moved in for his own attack. He, like his partner, was well-skilled in the use of a knife and was an agile fighter. When Dane tried to kick at him, he managed to jump quickly out of the way. That did, however, give Dane time to get back on his feet. Dane reached for his gun, only to discover that it wasn't there. It had fallen from his holster while he was on the ground.

The Mexican who was still in the fight saw then that Dane was unarmed. Smiling, he made another lunge, which Dane managed to avoid. Then, as Dane twisted away, he thrust his fingers into his attacker's eyes.

The Mexican screamed and dropped his knife, and Dane picked it up. By now the other man had recovered from the kick in the groin, and he came at Dane in a second attack. He didn't know Dane was armed and therefore made no effort to cover himself. Dane twisted away from the Mexican, then counterthrust with his own weapon, burying it deep in his attacker's chest. He turned the blade sideways so it would slide through the gap between the bones of his rib cage, then he twisted it, letting the Mexican tear himself off by his own weight, opening up a large, jagged wound. The Mexican's eyes opened wide in surprise. He dropped his own blade, struggled for a moment to pull the knife from his chest, then sank to his knees, and finally fell forward.

Quickly, Dane recovered his pistol and rifle from where he had dropped them. He turned toward the second man before he saw that he represented no threat. The second attacker was on his knees, both hands over his eyes, totally blinded by the fight. By now a dozen of more people had poured out of the saloon to see what was going on.

"Is there a sheriff in this town?" Dane asked.

"I'm the town constable," one of the men said.

"I had no choice. These men attacked me."

"Si, I saw it," Garcia, the young stableboy, said.

"They're a bad lot," the constable said. "They probably thought you had some money on you. Couple of you fellas want to carry that one down to the hardware store? McGinnis can put his body in a sack and we'll bury him tomorrow. I'll put the other one in jail."

"You are hurt," Carmen said, putting her hand on Dane's side. "Come, you can rest in my room. I'll put a bandage on your wound for you."

Dane followed Carmen back into the cantina, then up the stairs to her room. A couple of times on the way up, he had to lean against the wall alongside the stairwell, and when he did, he left his mark there, in blood.

At the top of the stairs, Carmen pushed open the door, then guided him over to her bed. He sat down, heavily, then winced as she stripped off his shirt. Working by the light that shone through the open door, she put her fingers on his wound.

"You are lucky, señor," she said. "The wound is not deep." She opened a door on the chifforobe and took out a petticoat, then ripped it into strips to be used for bandages.

"Did you know those two men?" Dane asked as she worked.

"Si. The one you killed was Antonio. The one you blinded is Miguel. They are very evil men, and they thought to steal money from you."

"No, they weren't after my money, Carmen, and you know it," Dane said.

Carmen looked at Dane in surprise. "Why do you say this thing?"

"You set me up," Dane said.

"I do not know what this means…set you up."

"As I was leaving the saloon, you said, 'Dane Calder, you must be very careful.' How did you know my name?"

Carmen didn't answer. Instead she continued to work in silence. Dane reached down and gripped her wrist tightly in his hand.

"I asked you a question, Carmen. I want to know how you knew my name?"

"Please, señor, you are hurting me," Carmen said as tears came to her eyes.

"Are you going to tell me what I want to know?"

"Si, si, I will tell you," Carmen said. "Please, let me go."

Dane released her wrist, and she rubbed it gingerly

"All right, talk," he ordered.

Carmen took a deep breath. "The men you are looking for, the ones led by the man with the evil eye, paid Antonio and Miguel to kill you. Then

Antonio and Miguel described you to me and told me you would be coming soon."

"I wonder how they knew I'd survived the dynamite," Dane said.

"Que?"

"They tried to kill me back in Thunder Ridge. I wonder how they knew they didn't do it."

"This, I do not know, señor."

"And you, Carmen. How much did they pay you to help them? Did they give you thirty pieces of silver?"

Carmen gasped, then quickly crossed herself. "Señor, you must not say such a thing! It is blasphemy. Besides, they paid me nothing," she said. "*Nada.*"

"Do you hate gringos so much that you would do this for nothing?"

"No, señor, that is not it. But, you see, Antonio and Miguel wanted to make sure they got the right man. So, they came to me and told me that I must find out who you were. It would be easy, they said, because I talk to all the men who come into the cantina. When I found out who you were, I was to say the name out loud. That is why I said, 'Dane Calder, you must be very careful.'"

"And what did you get for this?"

"As I told you, señor, I got *nada.*"

Carmen walked over to a corner of the room where in the dark shadows was a screen. She moved the screen and Dane saw a wizened old lady holding a tiny infant. Carmen took the baby from the old woman and held it to her cheek. Her eyes were filled with tears, and they glistened brightly in the ambient light that spilled in through the open door from the candle sconces in the hallway outside.

"They told me if I did not do this for them, they would kill my *abuela* and sell my baby. I am sorry, señor, but you must understand. I could not let anything happen to my family."

Dane sighed, then reached for his shirt. "All right," he said. "I understand."

"Where—where are you going?" she asked.

"After Cottrell and his men."

"But you are hurt. You must rest."

"I'm not hurt that bad," he said. "And lady, if I chose to rest here, I might be resting for an eternity. No, ma'am. I think I'd be a lot better off gettin' me a room over at the hotel."

"You are wrong about me," Carmen said. She shook her head. "I would not betray you now. I had no choice before, but I would not do it now."

Dane nodded his head. "Thanks for the bandages," he said, as he started for the door.

"Dane Calder," Carmen said in barely a whisper. When Dane stopped, she went on. "Be careful. When they find out Antonio and Miguel did not kill you, they will find others."

Dane grinned wryly. "I'm sure they will," he said.

"But that is very dangerous for you," Carmen

cautioned. "How will you know who is your enemy and who is your friend?"

"That's easy," Dane said. "I have no friends."

CHAPTER 6

THE NIGHT CREATURES SERENADED EACH OTHER AS Morgan Cottrell and the others waited just outside Vista del Sol. A cloud passed over the moon, then moved on, bathing the little town in dull silver. From there, they could hear the distant ringing sound of a guitar and the high bleat of a trumpet, a counterpoint to the melody of the owls. It had been nearly an hour since they sent Parish into town to find out what happened.

"Where the hell is he?" Al asked, pacing nervously in the darkness. "He said he'd come back soon as he found out what happened."

"Do you think them two hombres killed him?" Gus McMein asked.

"Yeah, sure they did," Al answered hopefully. "I mean, hell, they was two of 'em wasn't they? And Calder wouldn't have been on the lookout for them."

"You don't know Dane Calder," Morgan said. "He's always on the lookout."

"Yeah, but what I mean is, he's just one man. And he's human, just like ever'one else."

"'Ceptin' we already know he didn't get hisself killed in that dynamite blast," Tim added. "He's comin' after us, Al. Mark my words, he's comin' after us. Especially you, 'cause you pissed him off back there when we was in the jail together." Tim giggled.

"Damn you!" Al said, angrily. "What's the matter with you? Somebody ought to shoot your other ear off. He's coming' after you too, or don't you know that?"

"Would you two just hush your damned bickerin'?" Morgan hissed. "Someone's comin'."

The four men got into position behind rocks and cocked their pistols, then waited. A moment later they recognized Parish, not by his features, it was much too dark for that, but by the way he was sitting on his horse.

Parish rode into the camp and dismounted, then he tossed a full bottle of whiskey toward the group.

"Thought you might like this," he said.

"Thanks," Tim said, pulling the cork. He smelled the liquor, then turned it up and took several long swallows before he passed it on to the next man.

"Well?" Morgan asked anxiously, his wandering eye flashing as brightly as the other.

"Got any coffee left?" Parish asked, walking over

to the glowing coals. He found a tin cup and filled it with coffee from the blue pot that sat on a stone near the fire. He took a couple of swallows, then wiped the back of his hand across his mouth. "That's good," he said.

"Dammit, Parish, what the hell happened?" Morgan demanded.

"Nothin'," Parish answered.

"Nothin'?"

"Well, nothin' that was good for us. Calder blinded one of them Mexicans, and he killed the other one. Let me tell you somethin', in case you ain't figured it out yet. That man takes a heap of killin'."

Morgan kicked at the dirt. "I should've known better. I should've known better than to hire a couple of Mexicans to do the job. I gave 'em twenty dollars apiece, and for what? Nothin', that's what. The forty dollars is gone and Calder is still on our trail."

"Well, hell, Morgan, it ain't like as if they didn't try to kill him," Tim said. "One of 'em got hisself killed tryin'."

"Yeah? Well, as far as I'm concerned, they didn't try hard enough," Morgan insisted.

"What are we goin' to do now?" Al asked, his voice reflecting his fear. "He's comin' after us. We can't just sit around waitin' on him, can we?"

"I don't know, I don't know," Morgan said. "I'll think of somethin'."

"Maybe we won't have to think of nothin',"

Parish suggested. He took another drink of coffee, showing an amazing amount of calmness, compared to the others. "Maybe it's goin' to be done for us."

"What? What are you talkin' about?"

"Did you know Vess Akers?" Parish asked. "He come out here from Texas a couple of years ago."

"Yeah, I know him," Morgan said. "I haven't run across him in a while, but I know him. Why you askin'?"

"You ain't run across him lately 'cause he's dead," Parish explained. "Calder killed him. Shot him down about four or five weeks ago, for the two-hundred-dollar reward." Parish chuckled.

"Why do you find that funny?"

"While I was back in town there, I seen three men at the saloon. I thought maybe I know'd 'em from somewheres, so I just sorta hung back and listened in on 'em. Seems one of them is Akers's brother; the other two is his cousins. They been doggin' ol' Calder's trail all the time he's been chasin' us. What do you think of that?"

"So what?" Morgan asked.

"So what? Why, them boys is hangin' aroun' town tonight," Parish said. "First thing tomorrow mornin', they're plannin' on killin' ol' Dane Calder."

———

THERE WERE three men in the livery stable when the sun came up the next morning. One was a small man with a high forehead and weasel eyes. That was

Gil Akers. The other two were his cousins, Murray and Chance Coleman. Both were larger men than Gil, though it was obvious that Gil was in charge. Murray had a handlebar mustache; Chance wore a full beard. Actually there was a fourth man in the stable, or rather, a boy, for Garcia, the stableboy, was sitting in the corner, bound and gagged.

"You're sure he's still in town?" Murray asked.

"That's his horse, ain't it?" Gil said, pointing to Dane's mount.

"That's what the boy said," Murray replied.

"Well, he sure ain't gonna be leavin' town without it, is he?"

"No, I don't reckon," Murray answered.

Chance carved off a piece of chewing tobacco and slid it in his mouth, barely discernible under his beard. He put the plug away without offering any to any of the others. "Too bad them Mexicans didn't get him last night," he said.

"If you ask me, I'm just as glad them two didn't get him," Gil replied. "I'd a heap rather do it myself. It was my brother he killed."

"Yeah, well, I don't mind helpin' you kill'im," Murray said, stroking his mustache. Murray was sitting on a bag of oats, leaning against the stall. "But I hope you ain't plannin' on callin' him out or nothin' like that. I mean, I think the best thing to do is just wait for him in here and then start blastin' away the moment we see him. We ought to just shoot him down before he even knows what's goin' on."

"That's just what we're goin' to do," Gil said. He looked over at his two cousins and smiled. "After all, I ain't tryin' to make no name for myself or nothin'. I just want to kill 'im for killin' Vess. An eye for an eye, a tooth for a tooth, and a life for a life. Just like it says in the Good Book."

Murray laughed. "Your pappy, Uncle Eli, bein' a preacher an' all, sure wouldn't take too kindly to you usin' the Bible to justify your killin'."

"Why not?" Gil replied. "They's lots of killin' in the Bible." He walked over to the open window to look down the street toward the hotel. Dane was coming through the front door at that very moment, walking slowly and stiffly because of the wound in his side. Gil chuckled.

"What is it?" Murray asked. "What do you see out there?"

"Well, now, lookee here, lookee here," Gil said. "Looks like ol' Dane Calder is comin' right to us. You boys get ready."

"We're goin' to just shoot 'im, ain't we, Gil?" Murray asked. "I mean, remember what you said about not bracin' him or anything."

"I ain't gonna brace him," Gil said. He looked at the other two men. "But I get the first shot."

"Hell, that's okay by me," Murray said.

"Yeah, me too," Chance agreed.

As Dane approached the stable, he saw a bird start inside, then wheel around just before it reached the shadows, and fly away. If any one of a thousand other men had seen that same thing, it would have meant nothing. It was only that one in a thousand, the man who lived his life on the edge, keenly attuned to the slightest nuance, who would notice something unusual about the bird's behavior.

Dane showed absolutely no reaction to what he had observed but kept walking until he had walked right on past the stable.

———

"What the hell?" Chance asked. "Where'd he go?"

"Maybe he's goin' down to have hisself some breakfast first," Murray suggested. "Where is he, Gil? Do you see him?"

"I don't know where he is," Gil answered.

"And I can't get no closer to the door to have a look-see, 'cause if I do, he might see me."

"Damn. Why didn't he come on in here like he was supposed to?"

"Maybe he seen us?"

"How the hell could've he seen us? We was all back in the shadows."

"Well, he seen somethin'."

"No, he didn't," Gil said. "I'm sure he just went to breakfast. He'll be back in a few minutes. All we got to do is wait for him."

———

As soon as Dane reached the corner, he turned, then, shielded by the buildings, moved quickly toward the rear of the livery stable. He climbed up on the fence, then grabbed a rope that hung down from the hay lift and, using it, pulled himself up into the loft. The exertion hurt his side, and once he was up in the loft, he had to stand very still for a moment, holding his side until the pain subsided. He felt around to make certain that the wound wasn't bleeding again and was gratified to learn that it wasn't.

Slowly, quietly, Dane began moving across the straw-covered floor of the hayloft. It was dark up there, but enough morning light splashed in through the open doors for him to see below. When he reached the edge of the loft, he saw that there were three men with drawn guns watching the front door. He drew his pistol and cocked it.

"Are you men looking for me?" he said calmly.

"It's Calder, in the loft!" Gil shouted. Gil fired a shot, even as he warned the others. His gun flashed and boomed, but the bullet wasn't even close enough for Dane to hear its buzz. Dane fired back, and an ugly hole appeared in Gil's forehead as a spray of yellow-gray brain tissue exploded from a bigger hole in the top of his head. Gil pitched back, dead before he even hit the ground.

Of the other two, Murray was in a better position to return fire, but even as Dane was shooting

Gil, he was already selecting his next target. Dane fired at Murray, hitting him in the shoulder, knocking him down and sending his gun flying. Chance finally managed to get into position to get off a shot before Dane turned on him, but Chance's shot whizzed by, then thocked harmlessly into one of the rafters just overhead. Dane's third bullet caught Chance in the leg, and Chance yelled, then dropped his gun as he covered the hole with his hands. Dane had both men down and unarmed now, while he stood in the loft, looking down at them.

"Who the hell are you?" Dane asked.

"That there was Gil Akers," Chance said, pointing to the dead man. Chance's voice was strained with pain. "He was Vess Akers's brother."

"We're his cousins," Murray added. Murray was clutching his shoulder wound. "Gil come to get us to help him get even with you."

"You still plannin' on helpin'?" Dane asked.

Chance looked over at his cousin, who was lying dead on the floor.

"Mister, far as I'm concerned, them two brothers is eatin' breakfast together in hell, right now," he said. "I don't want no more part of it."

Dane climbed down from the loft, then noticed for the first time, that Garcia was tied up. He walked over to untie him, finishing just as the town constable and a handful of others come to investigate the shooting.

"You again?" the constable said.

"This was not Señor Calder's doing," Garcia explained. "These three hombres were waiting for him, Señor Constable. They wanted to kill him."

"Calder, you better watch out," the constable said. "Looks to me like you're likely to be runnin' out of bullets before you run out of enemies."

"Could be," Dane said. "Could be."

"Come on, you two," the constable said. "You're goin' to jail."

"We need a doctor," Chance complained.

"Ain't got a real doctor," the constable said. "If the barber gets time, I'll send him over to the jail a little later to have a look at you." He looked at Dane. "I hope you're leavin' town. You seem to be fillin' up our jail and our graveyard."

Dane threw his saddle over his horse and tightened down the cinches. "I'm on my way," he said.

CHAPTER 7

IT WAS SEVEN DAYS AND TWO TOWNS LATER, AND
Dane didn't know the name of either. It was late
afternoon and the sun was a brilliant red orb, disk
high above the western horizon, when Dane first
saw the little town clustered on the side of a mountain in front of him. A shimmer of red sunlight
bounced off the roofs and clapboard sidings of the
dozen or so buildings that made up the town.

This was a mining community, and a little higher
up, above the buildings of the town, zigzagging
wooden trestles filigreed the face of the mountain.
White wisps of steam feathered out of the vents of
the press mill, and its cylinder steam pipe boomed
loudly, as though the place were under a cannonade.
Boiling out of the high smokestack was a large
plume of black smoke, its sulfurous odor permeating
the entire valley.

Dane's horse, realizing that he was near the end

of his day's journey, picked up the pace slightly as they rode into the town.

A kiosk in the middle of the street advertised Iron Cactus Saloon for Beer, and Dane thought that sounded like a pretty good idea. He would have a beer, but not before he had taken care of his horse. He had learned long ago that his mount came first, not from sentimentality or from affection for the critter, but from practicality—the health of his horse could mean the difference in his own survival.

A few minutes later, with his horse boarded at the livery, Dane crossed the street and walked down the boardwalk, passing a handful of buildings until he came to the Iron Cactus Saloon. A large sign touting the establishment hung over the boardwalk, squeaking an invitation as it rocked in the evening breeze. Right under the swinging sign was another sign, nailed to the wall alongside the door. This was a big picture of a beer mug, golden yellow at the bottom, white foam at the top. It was actually for those who couldn't read, but it also had the effect of appealing to those who could, for Dane literally licked his dry lips as he passed it on his way inside.

A half-dozen men and one woman were inside the saloon. There were three particularly large men sitting together at one of the tables. Dane glanced over at them and saw that they weren't cowboys. Remembering the mine he had seen while he was riding in, he realized that they must be miners.

The one woman in the place was sitting in a chair by the wall where a piano would be if there had been a piano. The Iron Cactus was like so many of the establishments that grew up around the mines, however, this saloon did not want to pay to have a piano shipped out, and then pay someone to play it.

The woman, seeing someone new come into the bar, smiled broadly and walked over to meet him. Dane guessed that she was in her early thirties, though her face was older and her eyes were ancient.

"Buy me a drink, mister?"

"Sure, why not?" Dane said.

"My name's Rosa. What's yours?"

Dane remembered how he was set up by the young Mexican girl in Vista del Sol and he wondered if the same thing was happening here.

"Names don't much matter," he answered.

"You're new in town, aren't you? Come to work the mines, or to do your own prospecting?"

"You might say I'm prospectin'," Dane replied. "I'm lookin' for five men. The leader of the group is a mean-lookin' fella, with one eye that sort of stares off into space."

"Can't say as I've seen anyone that fits that description," Rosa answered. "But I'll be glad to keep an eye open for him and tell him you're lookin' for him if I run into him."

Dane chuckled. "Don't reckon you'll have to tell him," he said. "He knows I'm lookin' for him."

"There are five of them, you say?"

"Yes. Morgan Cottrell, Tim Tyrell, Al Santos,

Gus McMein, and Simon Parish. Ever heard of any of 'em?"

"Sure, I've heard of Morgan Cottrell," Rosa said. She shivered. "From what I hear, he's a bad one. You run with him?"

"Not exactly. Runnin' after him is more like it."

"Lawman, or bounty hunter?"

"Does it make any difference?"

"Not to me," Rosa said. "But I don't know anything about them, anyway."

"Anybody else?" Dane asked aloud. The others in the saloon turned toward him. "I'm looking for Morgan Cottrell, or any of his gang." He named them again. "I'd be much obliged if anyone could tell me anything about them."

The three miners looked at each other, nodded once, then got up to leave.

"How about you men? You know anything about them?" Dane called to them.

"No," one of them replied in a short, gruff voice. "We don't know nothin'."

"Not very friendly," Dane said to Rosa.

"Don't worry none about them," Rosa said. "They're hard-rock miners and ever'one knows their heads are as hard as the rock they work with."

Dane had a few drinks in the saloon then he ate supper in the Horseshoe Café. After that, he spent the rest of the evening trying to find out if anyone had seen Morgan Cottrell. Either no one knew anything, or no one was talking. But that wasn't unusual, Dane knew. Morgan Cottrell was not the kind of man anyone would want for an enemy, and giving information might very well put a person in that category.

Rosa had asked if he was a lawman or a bounty hunter. She'd told him it didn't make any difference to her, but Dane also realized that there was a certain degree of animosity toward him and his profession. Everyone wanted the outlaws caught and eliminated, but no one wanted anything to do with the men who handled that unpleasant task. In the degree of social acceptance, a bounty hunter was not much better off than the outlaw he brought in.

That didn't really bother Dane. He didn't give a damn about people anyway.

It was just after supper when he walked over to the stable to check on his horse and the three men accosted him. They were the same three who had walked out of the saloon earlier in the evening. Even if Rosa hadn't told him what they were, he would have known just by the way they looked. They were men who worked with steel and rock, and as a result they had massive shoulders and muscular arms.

They appeared suddenly and unexpectedly, stepping out of a stall just as Dane went into the livery. One of them went over to the barn door and pushed it shut.

"Well, hello again. You wouldn't talk to me in the saloon," Dane said. "Have you changed your minds?"

The two men in front of him spread their feet

apart and let their arms hang loosely by their sides. They grinned, somewhat obscenely, at Dane.

"What about it, Val? He wants to know if we've changed our minds."

"I ain't changed my mind, Eb. How 'bout you, Cletus? You want to talk to this fella?"

"Talkin' ain't exactly what I was plannin' on," Cletus said from behind.

"I get the idea this isn't going to be very sociable," Dane said.

Though night had fallen, the livery was illuminated. The light was very dim though, coming from a couple of kerosene lanterns that hung from nails on the supporting pillars in the middle of the barn. The two lanterns spread a soft, golden glow on the walls, the stalls, and even on the faces of the three men.

"Since you aren't in the mood for sociable conversation, is there somethin' else I can do for you three fellas?" Dane asked, tensing his muscles, prepared for whatever they had planned for him.

"Yeah," Cletus answered. Cletus was the one behind him. "You can shuck that pistol belt."

"Why would I want to do that?"

"'Cause, iffen you don't, I'm goin' to open up your spine with this double-barreled, ten-gauge Greener."

Dane heard the deadly metallic click of the two hammers being cocked.

"If you're goin' to shoot me with that shotgun

you don't need me to drop my holster. Just go ahead and do it," Dane said.

One of the two miners who was standing in front of him smiled, causing his teeth to gleam yellow in the flickering light. This was Val, the only one who was wearing a beard.

"You know what? I like you, mister," Val said. "You got guts, and I wouldn't want to have anything to do with a man who didn't have guts."

"Only, we ain't being paid to kill you," Eb said. "Just beat you up some."

"Beat me up?" Dane asked, puzzled by the statement. "I can't see Morgan Cottrell paying anyone to beat me up. I figure he wants me dead, not whipped."

"Well, then, there you go. You see, Morgan Cottrell ain't got nothin' to do with this. This here comes from a man name of Parish."

"Simon Parish?"

"Uh-huh. He gave up ten dollars each to take you down a peg or two. He says to tell you it's for what you done to him in Thunder Ridge."

Dane unbuckled his gun belt and let it drop. "Yeah, I guess I did knock him around, a little," he said. He chuckled. "Is that what this is all about?"

"Mister, I don't know what you got to laugh about," Val said. "We're about to beat the hell out of you."

"Then you don't mind if I start first?" Dane asked, and catching the miners off guard by his unexpected move, he hit Val in the nose with a short but powerful punch.

"That hurt, you——" Val shouted. Blood spewed out of his nose down into his beard.

From behind him, Cletus suddenly hit Dane right between the shoulder blades with the butt of his shotgun. Dane felt the explosion of pain go all the way through his body. His knees buckled, and he thought for a moment that he might vomit.

Dane let out a loud, air-expelling *ooof* and fell forward, reaching out with both hands to try and steady himself. As he did so, Eb caught Dane with a solid, right-hand punch on the point of his chin, and Val recovered enough to send a club-like blow to the side of Dane's head, striking him just on the ear and making his head ring. Dane saw stars, and he could feel torn flesh on his ear from the effect of the punch.

The three miners relaxed a little. Each of them figured that they would be Dane Calder's match, even if they were on their own. With three of them throwing punches, this wasn't exactly a fight, at least, not in their minds. To them it was more like a task, like excavating so many tons of rock.

"You two stand back and let me have 'im. I figure I owe 'im," Val said. Obligingly, the other two did stand back, but before Val could deliver his punch Dane managed to recover and sent a whistling punch right into Val's solar plexus. Val's face turned blue as all the breath was expelled from his body, and he staggered back, grabbing his stomach. Dane stepped toward him and threw another right hand straight into his already broken nose. This time he felt the nose go under his hand, and if Val had had any breath, he would have yelled out again. As it was, he just fell, like a poleaxed steer, the flow of blood from his nose now restricted by the crushed cartilage.

With an angry yell, Cletus and Eb closed in on Dane, and though he tried to fend off their punches, the powerful fists of the two men fell on him like blows from a sledgehammer. Even when he was able to deflect the punch away from his face and catch it on his arm or shoulder, the blows were powerful enough to numb his arm. He was afraid that too many more such punches would render him completely helpless.

He finally realized that it was useless to try and ward off the miners' punches. So while he still had the strength and the control of his limbs, he figured his only chance was to get in as many of his own punches as hard and as fast as he could. He managed to score a telling blow to the eye of one of them and, a moment later, landed a punch to the mouth of the other, feeling a couple of the man's teeth crack under his fists.

Despite Dane's best efforts, however, he was unable to hold them off. Blow after blow was rained on him until he reached the point where he could no longer fight back. All he could do was draw himself up into as tight a ball as he could and take the pummeling. Finally, even that effort failed to protect him, and he went down. When he did, the miners began kicking him.

"That's enough, that's enough," Eb said. "We ain't gettin' paid to kill him, and I ain't doin' no more'n we're gettin' paid for."

"What are we goin' to do with 'im?"

"Just leave him here."

"What about Parish?"

"What about him?"

"Shouldn't we tell him what we done?"

"Why should we? He's done paid us already. As far as I'm concerned, I'm done with it."

Cletus spit out a tooth. "You got to hand it to the feller. He put up a fight, didn't he? I'll be spittin' teeth for a week."

"Come on, let's get Val and get out of here."

While the two miners helped Val to his feet, Dane lay without moving in the dirt on the floor of the barn between two long rows of stalls. He waited to get up until he heard the door open and close as the three miners left. But he found that he was unable to stand. His side felt wet and sticky and when he put his hand there, he felt blood. He knew that the knife wound had been opened up again. Exhausted, he lay back down, sucking in air in heavy, audible gasps.

One of the horses whickered.

From the saloon across the street, he heard the high-pitched trill of a woman's happy scream, then the heavy peal of a man's laughter.

An unseen rider passed by just outside the livery

barn, and Dane could hear the hollow clopping of the horse's hooves. In the outside world, life was going on as normal, while in the barn Dane was fighting just to stay conscious.

Painfully, laboriously, Dane tried again, and he began pulling himself across the dirt floor to the nearest stall. Using the boards of the stall for leverage, he finally managed to work himself into an upright position. It was another few minutes before he was able to work up the strength to stand. The effort was exhausting, however, and once up, he had to lean onto the stall for several moments while he recovered his breath.

The first thing he worried about was whether or not any bones were broken. Slowly, he began a system of self-examination checking his ribs, collarbone, arms, legs, and fingers. Finally he was convinced that, though badly bruised, he had no broken bones. Nevertheless, he had to admit that, of all the fights he had been in, this was, without a doubt, the most severe beating he had ever taken.

The door to the livery opened, and Dane tensed. He started to reach for his gun, then realized that his holster was still lying where he had dropped it earlier. If someone was coming to kill him now, it would be little more than an execution. Maybe this was what Parish had in mind when he hired the miners in the first place. Slowly, and as quietly as he could, Dane managed to move back into the darker shadows.

"Dane? Dane, are you in here?"

It was Rosa.

"Dane?"

Was this another setup? Or was she genuinely concerned about him? Finally, Dane decided that he would have to take a chance.

"I'm over here, Rosa," Dane called, quietly. "Behind the stall."

Rosa closed the door behind her then walked quickly, over to him.

"Oh, my," she breathed when she saw him. She pulled a handkerchief from the cuff of her sleeve and dipped it into one of the water troughs, then dabbed it against a cut on his forehead. "They nearly killed you."

"How did you know I was in here?" Dane asked.

"Those three came back to the saloon, bragging about what they had done," Rosa explained. "But from the looks of things, it's no brag…it's all fact."

"How did they look?" Dane asked.

Despite herself, Rosa chuckled. "Not pretty," she said. "Not nearly as bad as you, mind, but not pretty. Why did they do this?"

"They were just deliverin' a message, that's all," Dane said. "From an old friend."

"Some friend," Rosa said as she continued to work on him.

"Yeah. Now I owe him one."

CHAPTER 8

THE NOISE IN HIS HEAD SOUNDED LIKE THE INSIDE OF a drum. Dane opened his eyes and looked around. The room was lighted by the spill of early morning sunlight, and the air was scented by Rosa's musky perfume, though she was gone.

The drum sounded again, and this time Dane realized that it was someone pounding on the door.

"Yeah," Dane mumbled. "Yeah, just a minute." Dane swung his feet over the edge of the bed, feeling pain in every part of his body. Putting it out of his mind, he pulled his gun, then walked over to the door and jerked it open. A tall man with clear blue eyes and a long, sweeping mustache stood just in the hall. He was wearing a star pinned to his shirt.

"You're Dane Calder?" the man asked.

"Yes, I am. Why?" Dane asked.

"My name is Barnhill, Calder. I'm the sheriff of this town. I need your help."

Dane brushed his hair back from his face and even that gesture caused him to wince in pain.

"Help?"

"There's a couple of men holed-up down at the saloon. They broke into it early this morning, and when I went down there to run them off, they said they would kill me if I came back."

Dane walked over to the dry sink and poured a pan of water from the large pitcher. He began washing his face, then reached for the towel and dried himself before he answered.

"Well, you're the sheriff," he finally said. He reached for his shirt. "Seems to me those kind of threats go with the badge."

"I ain't denyin' that," Sheriff Barnhill answered. "But that don't mean I can't ask for a little help from time to time. What do you say, Calder? Will you help me? I mean it's right down your alley. There's paper out on both of 'em."

"Who are they?"

"A couple of hard cases. One's named Brady, the other is called Owens. Ever heard of 'em?" the sheriff asked.

"I don't know. I think I might've seen somethin' on them," Dane agreed. He stroked his chin. "But as I recall, they weren't worth enough for me to go after."

"Maybe they're not worth ridin' all over hell's half acre to look for. But they're here now, so there's no need for you to chase after 'em. And since I can't claim any of the reward, it'll all be yours. All I'm askin' is that you just give me a hand bringin' 'em in."

Dane sighed. "All right," he said. He pulled on his pants, then reached for his boots. "Give me a few minutes. I'll go down there with you."

"I appreciate it," the sheriff replied. He smiled wanly. "The truth is, I'm getting' a little old for this sort of thing. Breakin' up fights and runnin' in drunks is about all I'm good for anymore."

"Yeah?" Dane said, wincing as he buckled on his pistol. "Well, tell me, Sheriff, if you're so damned good at breakin' up fights, where the hell were you last night when I needed you?"

"I'm sorry about that, Calder," the sheriff replied. "I heard about what happened to you, but I didn't know nothin' about that until it was all over. If you want, I'll put them three men in jail, right now."

"No, leave 'em alone. There's no real harm done I reckon. They could've killed me, but they didn't," Dane said. He reached for his hat. "Let's go."

As Dane and the sheriff walked toward the saloon from the hotel, Dane saw that word of the impending showdown had already spread through the rest of the town. Men and women were already gathered in curious little groups on both sides of the street, talking quietly among themselves and looking anxiously toward the saloon, speculation as to what was about to happen.

Three of those who were gathered for the show were the miners who had beaten up Dane the night before. They were standing on the porch in front of the hardware store. Val had his nose bandaged; the other two were sporting black eyes and swollen lips. Despite himself, Dane couldn't help but smile. It looked as if he had managed to get in a few scoring punches of his own, after all. He waved at them and they, rather sheepishly, he thought, even waved back.

A shot suddenly rang out from the saloon, and a puff of dust flew up from the road. That was followed by the whining sound of a spent bullet.

"That's just about far enough, Sheriff!" someone called from inside the saloon.

"Brady, Owens, I want you two men to put your guns down and your hands up," Sheriff Barnhill called. "Then I want you to come walking out of there."

"We can't hardly do that. It's gone too far, now. I reckon if you want us, you're just goin' to have to come get us."

"Then I gotta tell you men, this here is Dane Calder," the sheriff said. "If I do have to come in for you, Calder will be comin' with me."

"Wait—wait a minute!" the voice called from inside. There was a moment of silence, then the voice called out again. "Sheriff, will you come in alone, just to talk things over?"

"Don't do it, Sheriff," Dane said quietly. "You got nothin' to gain by talkin' to 'em. Just tell 'em to come on out."

Sheriff Barnhill took off his hat, then wiped his face with his handkerchief. "I don't know, Calder.

Seems to me like my job is to try to settle this without shootin' if I can. I can't see that it would hurt anything just to go on in and see what they have to say."

"I wouldn't go in there if I were you," Dane said again. "I got a bad feelin' about this."

"Well, I reckon that's the difference between bein' a bounty hunter and a lawman," Sheriff Barnhill said. "You see, even if I was to have that feelin', I'd still have to try everything I could to settle it peaceable like." The sheriff took off his pistol belt and hooked it around the end of the hitching rail, then looked back at Dane. "Promise me you won't do nothin' to spook 'em?"

"I won't," Dane promised.

Sheriff Barnhill put his hands up in the air. "All right, you two men, I'm comin' in to palaver some with you," he called. "And, as you can see, I'm leavin' my gun behind."

Dane followed the sheriff to the corner of the saloon, then he stepped back into the alley with his gun drawn and waited. The sheriff clumped across the wooden porch, paused for a moment as if drawing a deep breath, then pushed through the batwing doors and went inside.

In the very next instant Dane heard a muffled gunshot, then he saw Sheriff Barnhill come back outside through the batwings. There was a peculiar glowing on his shirt, and Dane realized that it was a tiny circle of fire His shirt was burning!

"I'm killed, Calder," the sheriff said. The expression on his face and in his voice was one of disbelief. He made it to the edge of the porch, then he fell facedown into the alley. Dane rolled him over and patted out the ring of fire on his shirt. It was then that he realized the fire was caused by powder burn. Sheriff Barnhill had been shot at pointblank range. That was also why the gunshot sounded muffled.

Suddenly there was the sound of crashing glass, and Dane looked up to see a chair and a fountain spray of shattered pieces of glass, sun-glistening, as they flew out into the street. The chair and shower of glass were followed almost immediately by a man, leaping through the newly made opening.

"There goes one of 'em! He's gettin' away!" someone on the street called.

Almost concurrent with the warning shout, the man who had just jumped through the window turned and fired toward Dane. Dane dropped to the ground and rolled to his right, then fired back. His bullet hit the gunman in the leg, and Dane saw a tiny spray of blood and bone flying from the kneecap. The gunman let out a howl of pain and went down, but by now the second gunman had entered the fray, coming through the smashed window and diving for cover behind the watering trough in front of the bootmaker's shop, which was next door to the saloon.

By now the people on the street were screaming and running. Whereas a moment earlier they had all been jockeying for a view, now they were trying to get out of the way.

Dane, realizing that his own position was exposed, dived behind the edge of the saloon porch. It was a very low porch, so that the only way Dane could get any protection was to stay as low to the ground as he possibly could. Because of that, he was having a difficult time getting into position to fire. The outlaw behind the watering trough had no such problem, and he fired at Dane.

"Brady! Brady, why ain't you shootin'? Are you all right?" the man from behind the watering trough yelled.

"I'm hit, Owens. I'm hit really bad," Brady answered, his voice strained with pain.

"Where you hit?"

"In the knee."

"In the knee? Dammit, that don't mean you're dyin'! Shoot! Shoot at the bastard!"

Brady raised up and fired. His bullet dug a crease in the top of the board and sent a spray of splinters flying. Owens fired again, and his bullet came much closer than any of the others. It was so close that it knocked Dane's hat off.

Dane realized then that he couldn't stay where he was, so rising up and firing several shots to cover his move, he darted across the street and dived behind the long row of produce barrels that sat on the front porch of the general store. Once there, he began punching out the empty shell casings and reloading his gun. He looked out onto the street and saw Brady just lying there. Brady realized that he was a sitting duck.

"Calder!" Brady shouted. He put his gun down and put his arms in the air. "Calder, look at me! I'm puttin' my gun down here, do you see? I ain't in this fracas no more. You hear me? I ain't in this no more Don't shoot me!"

"You yellow-livered, low-down coward," Owens shouted. "*I'll* shoot you." Owens rose up and fired, and Brady went down with a bullet hole in his chest.

Dane, with his pistol reloaded, crawled along on his belly to the far edge of the barrels, then looked around, trying to find an opening for a shot. That was when he saw something that Owens hadn't noticed. Dane smiled.

Owens was across the street from Dane, lying behind the watering trough in front of the bootmaker's shop. In the window of the bootmaker's shop was a long, low mirror, turned at just the proper angle to show the feet of the people as they walked by. A sign over the mirror said "Check your boots. Do you need new ones?"

Though the mirror was set to show the feet of passersby, it was also at exactly the correct angle to show Owens, lying on his belly in the street, behind the watering trough.

Owens stuck his pistol around one edge of the trough and fired, then quickly he turned and started crawling down to the other end. It might have been a good ploy. His shot might actually have directed Dane's attention to the opposite end, had Dane not been able to see in the mirror everything Owens was doing. Dane watched as Owens inched along on his belly to the opposite end of the trough where he knew Owens's face was about to appear.

Slowly, Owens peered around the corner to see where Dane was and what was going on. Dane drew in a breath, then let half of it out and held it. When enough of Owens's head was exposed to give him a target, Dane squeezed the trigger. The pistol roared and bucked in his hand. A cloud of smoke billowed up, then floated away. When the cloud cleared, Dane saw Owens lying face down in the dirt with a pool of blood spreading out from under his head.

Dane stood up then and walked out into the middle of the street to look down at Brady. Bubbles of blood were oozing from Brady's mouth, and he was trying hard to breathe. His hands were clutched over his wound, and blood spilled out between his fingers.

Gradually the citizens of the town began coming out of their places of cover, from behind the corners of the buildings, out of stores, and even down from a few trees. Slowly, cautiously, they walked out into the middle of the street to where the three men lay shot.

"Is that one dead?" someone asked Dane. He was pointing to Brady.

"No," Dane answered.

"Then somebody get a rope!" someone else shouted. "Get a rope and we'll hang the bastard!"

"He's bad gut-shot," Dane said. "He won't live long enough for you to get the noose around his neck."

Brady tried to cough, and when he did, blood poured from his mouth.

"It wasn't the sheriff we was after you know," Brady rasped. "It was you we really wanted."

"Yeah," Dane answered. "I sort of figured that. What I don't know is why? I wasn't after you two."

"I know you wasn't after us. That's why Owens figured you wouldn't recognize us." Brady erupted into another fit of coughing. "Five hundred dollars," he finally said.

"Five hundred dollars?"

"That's how much Cottrell said he would pay us for killin' you."

"Looks like you came out on the wrong end of the bargain," Dane said, but Brady didn't hear him. Brady was already dead.

———

LATER, on the night of that same day, Morgan Cottrell and his men were gathered around a low-burning campfire, eating their meager supper of beans and coffee.

"What do you think happened to him?" Al asked. "Do you think they got him?"

"Those two galoots?" Morgan replied. "Hell no, they didn't get him. You can bet on that."

"But you told 'em you'd give 'em five hundred dollars," Al said. "Surely they'd do it for five hundred dollars."

"Would you do it for five hundred dollars?" Tim asked, shoving a spoonful of beans into his mouth.

"Me? Hell, no!" Al answered. "What good is five hundred dollars goin' to do me when I'm dead? Don't forget, he knows me. He was in the jail cell right next to me. He'd recognize me the minute he seen me. But now, Brady and Owens, why, they might have a chance, don't you think?" Al asked hopefully. He put his plate of beans, barely touched, aside.

"I'll tell you what I think," Tim said. "I think he's got you so scared that you're about to pee in your britches, that's what I think. You goin' to eat the rest of them beans?"

"Hell yes, I'm scared," Al said. "And so are you and so is ever'one else if they got any sense about 'em. The only thing is, I don't mind admittin' that I'm scared."

Tim raked Al's beans off onto his own plate and continued to eat, scarcely missing a bite.

"Maybe I am scared," Tim admitted. "But since there ain't a hell of a lot I can do about it, I ain't goin' to be goin' around cryin' about it all the time." After about three more bites of his supper, Tim put the plate down, rather disgustedly. "Hell, Al, your beans don't taste any better'n mine."

"Did you think they come from a different pot?" Gus asked, laughing.

Tim twisted around to look at Morgan. "Dammit, Morgan, what's the sense of havin' money if we can't spend none of it? You know what

I'd like to do? I'd like to go into a town somewhere, have me a big steak and some fried taters an' onions, a beer or two, and maybe even a woman."

"You know we can't take the time to stop in a town right now," Morgan said. "Calder's too close on our tail."

"What if we go where he's already been?" Parish asked.

"What are you talkin' about?"

"Well, suppose we go back to that little mining town? You know he's been there by now, and one of two things will have happened. He'll either have been there and gone already, or…"

"Or what?" Al asked.

"Or he'll be dead, and we'll owe Brady and Owens five hundred dollars," Parish suggested.

Morgan thought about it for a moment, then he smiled broadly.

"Damn me if I don't think you've got a pretty good idea there," Morgan said. He laughed and slapped his knee. "First thing tomorrow mornin' we'll break camp and double back. We may as well go into town and let off a little steam."

———

IT WAS MIDMORNING when the five outlaws rode into town the next day. They rode right down the middle of the street, their hands next to their guns, ready on a moment's notice to react to anything that might challenge them. There were a lot of people in town, but none of them seemed to be paying any attention to Morgan or his men. In fact, it was almost as if they hadn't even been noticed.

"There's somethin' funny goin' on here," Morgan said. "Nobody's givin' us a second glance."

"There's the problem," Gus said, pointing. "There's somethin' down there in that store window. See, ever'one's gathered around it."

"Let's just mosey on down there and see what it is," Morgan suggested.

They rode through the town still, for all intent, unobserved. When they got close enough to see what was in the front window of the store, Al gasped. "Well, will you look at that!" he said.

They saw what had arrested everyone's attention. In the window of the hardware store were three coffins. All were shining black with polished silver fittings. The coffin lids were of the split type, with the bottom half closed and the top half open.

Lined with white satin, the coffins were propped up at a forty-five-degree angle, so that everyone passing by the window could clearly see not only the coffins but their contents as well.

There was a body in each coffin, pasty-faced, blue-lipped, and still. The sheriff's body was separate from the other two. His coffin was banked and surrounded by flowers, expressions of grief and respect from the town folk A sign over the sheriff read:

KILLED IN THE LINE OF DUTY

SHERIFF MARCUS W. BARNHILL

A BRAVE MAN

There was a sign over the other two men as well. It read:

THE OUTLAWS BRADY AND OWENS

NO FIRST NAMES NEEDED

THEY ARE

UNMOURNED AND UNMISSED

KILLED BY DANE CALDER

NOTORIOUS BOUNTY HUNTER

"Damn, look at *that*," Al moaned, pointing toward the window.

"What the hell, Al? Are you going to let on that you ain't never seen a dead man before?" Tim grumbled.

"I ain't talkin' about that," Al said. "I'm talkin' about that little sign, down there in the corner. Look what it says."

Morgan saw the sign that Al was referring to. Obviously hand lettered, it sat unobtrusively over in the corner, unseen by all but the most discerning.

MORGAN COTTRELL

I AM COMING AFTER YOU

CHAPTER 9

WHEN DANE FIRST CAME TO THE SOUTHWEST, HE was captured by a band of Apaches. Instead of killing him, the Indians, whose name means "enemy" took him in, making him a blood brother.

Eventually, Dane's band of Apaches fell afoul of a large detachment of the US Army. All were slaughtered except for Dane, who—wounded and dressed in Apache gear—feigned death. When the cavalry rode away from the killing ground, Dane's life as a loner, steeped in bloodshed, began in earnest. Dane had learned many things from the Indians, especially the art of tracking.

In describing Dane's tracking skills, a learned man once said that his Apache apprenticeship and his life as a hunter and huntee was the frontier equivalent of graduating summa cum laude from Harvard Law School and proceeding directly to the robe chambers of the chief justice of the Supreme Court.

Despite his skill as a tracker, Dane was having a difficult time at this moment believing what the trail was telling him. According to the signs, Morgan Cottrell and his gang had doubled back on their trail. The question was, were they really starting back or were they just trying to throw him off track? Dane was reasonably sure that wherever Morgan had gone, he would return to his original trail. That being the case, he decided to wait for them.

Just before nightfall, Dane rode onto a high bluff and dismounted, then looked west toward the setting sun. One of the secrets he had learned was that at dusk the trail dust from a horse could give off a glow that might be seen for miles. Dane looked for it but saw nothing. Below the bluff ran a gleaming thread of gold named the Engano River. Its name meant "mistake," and it was so named by the early Spanish settlers because it hadn't been on any of their maps.

The Engano was the only source of water for many miles around, and Dane knew that when the outlaws did come back, they would have to come back to this river. They would have no choice if they wanted to survive the wilderness. Dane turned away from his observation point, then walked back to his horse and untied his bedroll. He figured this was as good a place as any to spend the night.

————

DANE WAS AWAKENED EARLY the next morning by a series of whickers and snorts from his horse.

Evidently fleas or ticks were bothering him, and he was complaining about it. When it got light enough for him to see, Dane would pick them off. In the meantime the horse would just have to put up with it, though it was obvious from his snorting and complaining that he didn't like it.

Overhead the stars spread their diamond glitter across the heavens, while far in the east a tiny bar of pearl-gray light gave the first indication of the impending dawn. The wind, which had moaned and whistled across the hills and through the hollows all night long, was quiet now, and a predawn stillness had descended over the land. The only sound was the rippling flow of water from the Engano River.

Awake now, Dane picked up his bedroll and tied it behind the cantle. His pistol belt was hanging from the pommel, and he started to put it on but decided to have breakfast first. He pulled a piece of jerky from the saddlebag and took a bite, then wrapped it up and put it back. That was all the breakfast he would want or need.

Suddenly, with the sense of awareness developed by living with the Apache, Dane realized he was not alone. His first thought was to go for his gun, but as it was hanging from the saddle pommel, it would have been an awkward draw, and just as he knew he wasn't alone, he knew that he was being covered.

"Turn around," a low, menacing voice rasped, "and do it slow."

"With your hands up," another voice put in.

Dane turned to search the darkness for them,

but he could see nothing. Then he heard the sound of someone walking, and finally five men materialized out of the morning gloom. All five were holding guns. All five guns were pointing at him.

"Well now," Morgan said with a low chuckle. "Ain't this a lucky thing? Here we was just gonna get an early start this mornin', when we heard your horse stompin' around and carryin' on."

"Yeah," Al added, laughing. "You'd think a smart fella like you would have a horse that would know better."

"I seen the sign you left for me back in town," Morgan said. "The one you put in the hardware store window sayin' you was comin' after me."

"Did you?" Dane replied, speaking for the first time.

"I didn't like that very much," Morgan said. "In fact, I don't like you very much. You been ridin' our trail pretty hard and I'm gettin' damned tired of it."

"Yeah, well, that's what I do," Dane said.

"Well, you don't do it very good, do you? I mean, I thought you was supposed to be a smart tracker." Al giggled. "Only what happened? You got yourself caught by the same people you was tryin' to catch, that's what happened. That's a little like the rabbit catchin' the hound, ain't it?"

"If you say so," Dane replied.

"The funnin's over, Calder," Morgan said. He cocked his pistol. "I've been tryin' to have you killed, and there ain't noboby been able to get the job done. I guess that all goes to prove the old sayin' if you want somethin' done right, you gotta do it your-self. Boys, let's shoot the bastard and be done with it."

All the time Morgan and the others had been talking, Dane had been thinking. He remembered how, when they first accosted him, he hadn't been able to see them, yet they could see him. The reason he could be seen was because he had been standing by his horse, which was silhouetted against the sky. The reason he hadn't been able to see them was because Morgan and his men had approached from a dark background. Dane realized that if he could just move to his right, he would have the darkness of the hills behind him and he would be able to disap-pear in only a few steps. But the critical time would be in those first few steps. He needed an edge.

Suddenly Dane took a step to his left, even going so far as to throw his head and arms in that direction.

"Look out! His gun's on the saddle!" someone shouted, and all five outlaws swung their pistols that way, firing in the same motion. Even as they were firing, however, Dane had already reversed direction and was running back to his right.

The muzzles' flares lit up the darkness with bril-liant flashes as they fired, and the brightness had the effect of temporarily causing night blindness. As a result, Dane disappeared from their view even earlier than he thought he would.

"Where is he? What happened to him?" Morgan shouted in rage and frustration.

"I can't see a damned thing!" Parish complained, rubbing his eyes.

"Shoot! Shoot him!" Morgan roared.

The five guns fired a second time, but by now the men had no idea where he was and were shooting blindly. Dane reached the edge of the cliff, then launched himself into the black maw. He hadn't looked that closely at the river last night. He didn't know if he was plummeting toward a bloody and painful death on rocky cascades or to the relative safety of a deep pool. A second later the question was answered as he hit the water and went under.

There were no rocks. He had fallen cleanly.

Morgan and the others ran to the edge of the bluff and started firing down into the blackness below. As before, the orange flashes of their firing lit up the trees while burned powder and acrid smoke drifted up into their faces.

"Hold it! Hold it!" Morgan yelled. "We're just wastin' bullets here. We can't even see the bottom."

"How far down do you reckon that is?" Parish asked.

"Hell, I don't know. Maybe a hundred feet or more," Morgan answered.

"I bet he's dead," Al said. "Squashed flatter'n a pancake down there."

"Wait a minute. Throw a rock over," Morgan ordered. "You can get a pretty good idea how deep a hole is that way."

Parish picked up a rock and tossed it over, but it

was a relatively small rock and they didn't even hear it hit.

"That rock ain't hit yet!" Al said excitedly. "Hell, there ain't no tellin' how far down that is. The mighty bounty hunter is dead, sure'n hell."

"Kill his horse," Morgan said.

"Kill his horse? What the hell for?"

"Just kill the dammed horse like I told you to do," Morgan ordered. "If Calder did happen to live through that fall, then I at least want him to have to be on foot for a while."

"Yeah. Yeah, you got a point there," Al said. "I'll kill him."

Al walked over to the horse and raised his pistol, but the horse managed somehow to sense that something was wrong. He jerked his head up pulling loose from the ground hobble, while at the same time pushing Al back, knocking him off-balance. Free of his ground hobble now, the horse took off at a gallop.

"Hey!" Al called. "Come back here!"

"The horse is gettin' away, Morgan," one of the others said.

"Shoot 'im!" Morgan ordered. "Shoot 'im, dammit! Don't let him get away!"

Again, five guns blazed away, but they were no luckier at shooting Dane's horse than they had been at shooting Dane. Within a moment, the only sign of the horse was the clatter of his hooves echoing in the predawn darkness.

"He got away," Al said.

"I can see that you dumb…" Morgan said. "I should have done it myself."

"Yeah, well, it don't matter none anyway," Al said. "Calder's dead. This time he really is dead, ain't he, Morgan?"

"We'll hang around here until daylight," Morgan said. "Then we'll go down and look for him."

"What for? Why do we want to bother ourselves with lookin' for someone who's already dead?" Al asked. "We'd just be wastin' our time."

"I'd just like to make sure," Morgan answered.

———

DANE LET himself be carried about a mile downriver before he decided to come out, despite the fact that there were several times when he was swept painfully through rapids and across rocks. By the time he decided to leave the water he had so many cuts, bruises, and aches, he could no longer tell which injuries were old and which were new.

Dane swam toward the riverbank, then grabbed a tree limb. Slowly and painfully, he pulled himself out of the water, then crawled until he was on a relatively flat piece of ground. There, he fell on his back, exhausted from the effort and shaking with the cold.

Although Dane thought he had just closed his eyes for a moment, when he opened them again the sun was high and his clothes were nearly dry. He sat up with a start, then saw his horse calmly cropping grass not more than ten yards away. His rifle was still in the sheath, and his gun belt still hung from the pommel. He hadn't lost a thing.

———

MORGAN STOOD on a rock at the top of the pass, looking back over the path they had just traveled. From this vantage point he could see for many miles in every direction. They had stopped for a rest when they reached the top, supposedly to give the horses an hour or so to recover their wind, but in reality, to let Morgan have a long look around.

Behind him, his men were being entertained by a demonstration of Simon Parish's marksmanship. The sound of a pistol shot rolled down the mountainside, picked up resonance, then echoed back from the neighboring mountains. Parish turned the cylinder of his smoking pistol, pushed out the empties, and started shoving fresh loads into the chambers. He looked up at the others with a broad smile on his face.

"I'd like to see any one of you shoot like that," he said.

"Yeah, that was pretty good, all right," Tim agreed. "Better 'n anything I could do, or prob'ly any of the rest of us. But the only thing was, you was shootin' at a whiskey bottle, and it wasn't shootin' back. You run up on Calder, he's goin' to shoot back."

"Calder? What do you mean if I run up on Calder? He's dead," Parish said.

"No, I don't think he is," Tim replied.

"Why would you say that? You know he's dead. You was there, just like the rest of us. You seen 'im kill hisself by goin' over the edge of that cliff"

"I seen him go over the edge, just like the rest of you," Tim agreed. "But you might also recollect that come daylight, when we went down to look for him, we didn't find him."

"That don't mean nothin'," Parish insisted. "We all agreed that his body was prob'ly swept down river, that's all. Hell, some prospector will find his bones ten, twenty, maybe even a hundred years from now." He snorted. "They won't even know who he is."

"Yeah," Al put in. "He's dead, sure."

"No, he's not dead," Tim said. Tim raised his pistol and fired, breaking what was left of the empty whiskey bottle that had been Parish's target. "I don't think so, and Morgan don't think so either, do you Morgan?"

"Sure he does," Al insisted.

"No, he don't. That's why he's been lookin' for him."

Morgan climbed down off the rock and rubbed his chin, fixing all of them with the disconcerting, indirect stare that was caused by the wandering right eye.

"No," he finally said. "He ain't dead. He's still out there."

"How do you know?" Al asked. "Did you see him?"

"I don't have to. I can feel him," Morgan said.

"Morgan!" Al said, his voice dripping with fear. "You said you would kill him! You said we wouldn't have nothin' to worry about."

"I have to confess, I've never run across man or beast who took as much killin' as he does," Morgan replied.

"Well, I ain't waitin' no more," Al said. "I ain't just goin' to stand around and let him kill me anytime he wants. I'm getting' out of here."

"Gettin' out of here? What are you talkin' about?"

"I mean I'm runnin'," Al said. "I ain't ashamed to say that Calder has me spooked."

"You're runnin', are you?" Morgan asked. He chuckled. "Well now, s'pose you just tell us where it is you're a-runnin' to Al, and we'll all go with you. Dammit, man, don't you understand? We're not exactly invitin' him in to a social you know. We're tryin' to get away from him just as hard as we can. The only thing is, we don't have any place to go that he can't find us."

"Well, maybe if we'd split up, we'd have a better chance," Al suggested.

Tim laughed.

"What's so funny about that?" Al asked.

"If we split up he'll just track us down one at a time. That means we'll have to face him one at a time. Are you ready to face him all by your own self, Al?" Tim said.

"No! I mean, yes!" Al answered. "I mean, I'll face him if I have to."

"If you go out on your own, I guarantee you, you'll have to face him."

"Listen," Morgan said. "There's a nice fat bank down in Brimstone. I hear tell that they sometimes have as much as ten thousand dollars in it. If we was to knock that bank off, we'd have over twenty-five hundred dollars each, countin' what we also took back in Thunder Ridge. With twenty-five hundred dollars in our pocket, we could take a train to Denver, or San Francisco, or Kansas City, or some-place far off like that where Calder wouldn't be comin' after us. And when we got there, we could live fine for a long time. Long enough for Calder to give up on us."

"That sounds good to me," Tim said.

"Me too," Gus added, and Parish agreed.

"Al, it's just you," Morgan said. "Are you goin' along with the rest of us?"

"Yeah, I'll go along with the rest of you," Al said. "But I'm goin' to meet you in Brimstone, all right? I think I'd rather take my chances travelin' alone."

CHAPTER 10

DANE HAD JUST BIT OFF A CHEW OF JERKY WHEN THE crack of a rifle and the deadly whine of a bullet reached his ears simultaneously. He was lucky because he had just changed positions in the saddle at almost exactly the same moment the rifle was fired. Had he not done this, his head would have been where the bullet was.

Dane saw the white puff of smoke hanging just above a little knoll, some two hundred yards away. He leaned over the neck of his horse and urged it into a gallop, zigzagging as he advanced, but still covering the distance in less than fifteen seconds. He had his pistol drawn as he charged toward the smoke, and if so much as one eye peeked over the edge, he would shoot it out.

When he reached the knoll, he jumped from the saddle, then rolled behind a rock. From here he had an excellent view of the knoll, and he could even see a flash of light, the sun's reflection on the spent brass casing of the bullet that had been fired at him.

But that was all he could see, for there was no one there.

Dane lay behind the rock for a long moment until he was absolutely certain he was alone. Then he moved cautiously over to where his ambusher had been and picked up the brass casing. It was a .44-40, jacked out of a Winchester by the assailant after firing. There were also horse tracks nearby, and when Dane examined them, he saw that they were made by one of the horses he was trailing.

"Well," he said to himself. "So, I have flushed the covey into scattering, have I?"

The question was, of course, who was it? Morgan Cottrell himself, or just one of his men?

Dane swung back onto his horse and followed the tracks. The rider did everything he could to throw Dane off. He rode across solid rock, he tied brush to his horse's tail to rag out the tracks, he cut and re-cut his own trail, but Dane hung on.

Actually, Dane could have overtaken the rider and had it out with him then and there. He held back though, believing that despite the rider's attempts to confuse him, he might eventually lead him to the others.

When darkness fell that night, Dane saw the rider's campfire. He was pretty sure that it was a false campfire, set by the rider in hopes of luring Dane into an early camp, so he moved cautiously through the night until he reached it. When he looked around, he saw that he had been right. The rider hadn't camped at that spot and had no intention of doing so.

Dane continued on until he came to a range of steep, rocky hills. He was certain his quarry wouldn't try these in the dark, and even if he did, Dane wouldn't be able to follow his tracks. He decided, therefore, that the best thing for him to do was to stop and wait for the light of day.

————

FROM THE POSITION of the stars, Dane supposed that it was about two in the morning. He had been sleeping, but something awakened him. He lay quietly for a few minutes, listening to the sounds of the night. Wind sighed through the dry limbs of a nearby mesquite tree, and his horse whickered, but everything else was quiet. Still, something had awakened him.

Quietly, Dane moved away from his bedroll. He crawled over to a small depression, slipped down into it, and looked back at his bedroll. From here it looked as if someone was still in the blankets, and that was exactly the illusion he wanted to present.

Suddenly there was a flash of flame from a muzzle blast, followed immediately by the crack of a rifle shot. A puff of dust flew up from his bedroll, and Dane knew that if he had still been there, he would be dead now.

Dane waited to see if his nocturnal assailant

would follow up his ambush. There were no more shots and no one appeared. A moment later, Dane heard the sound of hoofbeats drumming against the hard, rocky ground. The rider was making a hasty retreat without checking to see whether he had killed Dane or not. Dane let him get away. If the rider thought Dane was dead, he might be less cautious and the trail would be easier to follow.

Dane's hunch was right; the trail was easier to follow the next day. In fact, he came within sight of his ambusher by midmorning.

————

AL LOOKED BACK over his shoulder and whipped his horse into a gallop as soon as he realized how close Dane actually was. Dane started galloping after him but stopped when he realized that all he was going to do was run his own horse into the ground. Then he saw a way to get an angle on the fleeing horseman. There was a long, narrow finger of a ridge that ran parallel with them, off to their right. The trail Al was following would take him around the far end of the ridge. Crossing over the ridge now would allow Dane to cut Al's trail, but there was a steep gulley on the other side of the ridge. It would be so difficult to negotiate that Dane wouldn't really gain enough of an advantage to actually catch Al. It would, however, give him the opportunity for a long-range rifle shot.

Dane turned his horse toward the ridgeline,

pushed him up to the top of it, then pulled his Winchester from the saddle sheath. He pulled the horse to a stop, then lifted his left leg and crossed it on the saddle in front of him, raised the rifle to his shoulder, leaned into it, and took a long, careful aim. He wasn't aiming at Al. He was aiming at Al's horse.

Dane took a deep breath, let out half his air, then slowly squeezed the trigger. The rifle roared and kicked back against his shoulder. He watched Al's horse run a couple more steps, then shudder, then go down on his forelegs. Al was tossed over his horse's head, and he rolled along on the ground for a few feet.

"I'm sorry, horse," Dane said under his breath as he put his rifle away. "You were just unlucky enough to have the wrong owner."

Dane urged his own horse forward, and within a few minutes, reached Al's side. Al was sitting on the ground, his arms wrapped around his legs, staring morosely at Dane as he approached.

"Hello, Al," Dane said easily.

Al glared up at him.

"You ain't human!" he said. "Can't you be killed?"

"Sure," Dane said. He cocked his pistol. "So can you, if you don't come with me now."

"Come with you? Where are you taking me?"

Dane pointed off to the north. "There's a town about six miles that way," he said. "I'm going to leave you in jail there, while I go after the others."

"How am I supposed to get there?" Al asked. "You killed my horse, remember?"

"Why, you're going to walk," Dane replied.

————

It made quite a sight as they entered town later that day. Dane was riding but Al was on foot. His hands were cuffed together, and he was being led by a rope.

"Hey, look at that! Look at the way than man is bringin' in that fella," someone shouted.

"Mister, who do you think you are? That ain't no way to bring in somebody." The protesting citizen ran down the sidewalk, his footfalls sounding loudly on the boards. "Ever'body, get out here an' take a look at this!" he called. "Look at the way this prisoner is bein' brought in."

From both sides of the street people began appearing, and they walked quietly alongside, watching with wide, curious eyes.

Dane stopped in front of the sheriff's office, then swung down from his horse.

"In there," he said gruffly, jerking on the rope to give Al his message.

The door to the sheriff's office opened, and the sheriff came out, then stood on the front porch, leaning against a post with his arms folded across his chest.

"Now, just you hold on there, mister," the sheriff

said. "Who the hell are you? And what do you mean, bringing someone in like that?"

"This is Al Santos," Dane answered, not giving his own name. "He's part of Morgan Cottrell's gang."

"Morgan Cottrell?" someone said.

"Hey, did you hear that? This here fella belongs to Morgan Cottrell's gang."

"Morgan Cottrell," someone else said, and the outlaw's name went from mouth to mouth, evoking expressions of fear and awe.

"Look here," the sheriff said. "Didn't Morgan Cottrell just break a couple of his men out of the Thunder Ridge jail by blowin' it up with dynamite?"

"Yep," Dane answered. He pointed to Al. "This was one of the men he broke out."

"Well, what are you doing bringing him here?"

"He's a wanted man, Sheriff," Dane said pointedly as if explaining something to a child.

"Not by me, he ain't wanted," the sheriff replied. "You want him in jail, you're gonna have to find someplace else to take him," the sheriff said. "I ain't gonna have my jail blowed up."

Al chuckled. "Yeah, yeah, now, that's real smart of you, Sheriff." He pointed at the sheriff with his cuffed hands. "I tell you what. You just be a nice fella and let me go. You do that, Sheriff, and I'll see to it that your jail ain't troubled none."

"He's worth two hundred dollars," Dane said, paying no attention to what anyone else was saying as he pushed Al toward the front door of the jailhouse. "So if you don't mind, I'd like you to send a wire off for whatever authorization you need to pay me the reward for this man. I'll be waiting in the saloon."

"Now just you hold on there!" the sheriff demanded angrily. "Mister, didn't you hear what I said? You ain't gonna put that man in my jail! And I damn sure ain't gonna pay you for him!"

"I can't put him in your jail?" Dane asked.

"No. Absolutely not!"

"You heard what the man said," Al said. "He don't want me in his jail."

"All right," Dane said, easily.

Al began chuckling.

Dane pulled out his pistol, put the barrel of it to Al's temple, then pulled back the hammer.

"Hey, what are you doing?" Al shouted in quick fear.

"Santos, you must've forgotten. It don't make any difference to me whether you are in jail or not. All I have to do is bring you in. I get paid the same whether you're dead or alive," Dane said. "So I think I'll just blow your brains out right here and now and be done with it."

"No, wait, are you crazy?" The sheriff gasped. One of the on-looking men also shouted out in surprise, and a couple of the women screamed.

"No, no don't shoot!" Al whimpered. "Please, don't shoot!"

"You better take that up with the sheriff," Dane said menacingly. "He either takes you in his jail, or I kill you here. And like I said, I don't care which one."

Al looked at the sheriff, his eyes pleading for help. "Sheriff, can't you see this man will do what he says? Please, let me stay in your jail!"

"Just a minute here," the sheriff said angrily. "You can't just threaten to blow a man's brains out, right in front of the whole town."

"Oh, it isn't a threat," Dane said easily. "I'd say it more like a promise."

"Just who the hell do you think you are, anyway?"

"The name is Calder. Dane Calder."

"Dane Calder?" someone said. There was a collective gasp from those who had gathered to watch, and now it was Dane's name that became a buzzing whisper passing from mouth to mouth until everyone knew that they were in the presence of the man who was also called *the* bounty hunter.

"Oh," the sheriff said, the bluster gone from his voice now. "Oh, well, why didn't you say so? Sure, Mr. Calder, I'd be glad to take care of your prisoner for you. And, of course, I'll pay you for it, just as soon as I get the authorization to draw the money from the bank."

"I'll be in the saloon," Dane replied, easing the hammer down on his pistol and putting it back in his holster. "Bring the money over there as soon as it comes in."

"Yes, sir, right away," the sheriff promised.

CHAPTER 11

THE SALOON WAS ON THE SAME SIDE OF THE STREET, about four buildings west of the jailhouse. A sign outside promised cool beer, and Dane thought that sounded pretty good. He stepped inside, then because it was so dark, he had to stand for a moment or two until his eyes had adjusted to the interior.

This was one of the nicer saloons he had been in for a while. The bar was made of burnished mahogany with a highly polished footrail. Crisp, clean white towels hung from hooks on the customer's side of the bar, spaced every four feet or so. A mirror was behind the bar, flanked on each side by a small statue of a nude woman, each statue set back in a special niche.

A row of whiskey bottles sat in front of the mirror, reflected in the glass so that the row of bottles seemed to be two deep.

Even the bartender was a part of the décor, with

slicked-back black hair and a handlebar mustache. He stood behind the bar, industriously polishing glasses.

"Is the beer really cool?" Dane asked.

The bartender looked up at him, but he didn't stop polishing the glasses.

"It's cooler than spit," he said matter-of-factly.

"In that case, I'll have one."

The bartender set the glass and towel down, picked up a mug, and held it under the spigot until it was full and foaming on top. He pushed it across the bar, and Dane put a coin down as he accepted it.

Dane drank the first beer for thirst, then ordered another one for pleasure. Then he turned to look out over the saloon. Three cowboys were playing cards for tobacco and matches at one of the tables, while a somewhat more serious game was going on at another. The rest of the people seemed to be interested only in drink and conversation.

At the table of the more serious game, one of the players got up and left.

"There's an open seat here," one of the remaining players at the table called out. It was an open invitation to anyone in the room who might be so inclined. "How 'bout one of you cowboys?" he offered.

"No, thank you, mister. I'm just playin' for matches and tobacco now and I'm losing my shirt."

The other cowboys at the table laughed.

"How 'bout you, mister? You want to play a little?" The invitation was made to Dane. Dane took another swallow of his beer, then wiped the back of his hand across his mouth before he answered.

"I might as well," he answered. He walked over to take the empty seat.

"Say, don't I know you?" one of the players asked, looking at Dane through narrowed eyes.

"I don't know," Dane said. "I don't know you."

"Broomfield's the name. Benjamin Broomfield."

"I don't know you," Dane said. He didn't give his own name.

"Weren't you down at the sheriff's office a while ago?" someone at one of the other tables asked Broomfield.

"No," Broomfield answered, counting out some chips for Dane. "Should I have been?"

"I don't know. But if you had been, you would know that this here fella is Dane Calder."

"Oh, are you *the* bounty hunter?" Broomfield asked, looking at Dane.

"Some call me that."

Broomfield ran the back of his finger across his lips and studied Dane for a long moment, as if deciding whether or not Dane was too dangerous to play cards with. Finally, he smiled.

"Well, what the hell?" he said. "I ain't got no wanted posters out on me. And as far as I know, neither do any of these other fellas." He slid the deck across the table. "Would you like to cut the cards, Mister Calder?"

"Thanks," Dane answered.

As Dane picked up the cards, he felt for

pinpricks, uneven edges, or rounded corners. Feeling none, he knew that the cards were honest. He'd know soon enough whether or not the players were.

————

"SHERIFF?" Al called. "Sheriff, you up there?"

The sheriff, who was reading a newspaper, sighed. "Yeah, I'm up here," he said. "What do you want?"

"I want a drink of water."

"You'll be getting' your supper soon," the sheriff replied, making no effort to answer his request. "You'll have water then."

"But I'm thirsty now."

"You ain't gonna die of thirst before suppertime."

"Come on, Sheriff. I had to walk purt' near six miles, you know. You seen how he brung me in, like I was an animal or somethin'."

The sheriff lay his newspaper aside and got up from his desk to walk over to the water bucket.

"All right," he said. "But I don't want to hear nothin' more out of you till suppertime. You got that?"

"Yeah, Sheriff. Thanks," Al said.

The sheriff scooped up a dipperful of water and carried it back to the cell. Al reached for it.

"Wait a minute, I'll have to turn the dipper to fit it through the bars," the sheriff explained.

"I don't care how you do it, just let me have it," Al said. "I'm pure dyin' of thirst."

The sheriff handed the dipper through the bars, but just as Al got his fingers on it, he let it drop. The dipper started to fall, spilling water on the sheriff's shirt.

"Damnit, Santos, look what you done. Why don't you be more careful?" the sheriff barked, making a grab for the dipper.

With the sheriff concentrating on the dipper, he wasn't as alert as he should have been, and that was exactly Al's plan. Al reached up and grabbed a handful of the sheriff's hair, then jerked his head forward, slamming it into the bars with a sudden, powerful, and totally unexpected move. The sheriff was knocked unconscious and fell to the floor, just outside the cell door. Al squatted down and reached out to retrieve the cell-door keys, which the sheriff was carrying on a ring on his belt.

A moment later, Al Santos was out of his cell, once again a free man.

Al jerked open a couple of drawers, looking for his pistol and holster, but he couldn't find them. Then growing concerned that someone might come in and find him out of the cell and rifling through all the drawers, he decided to just grab a shotgun down from the rack. He opened it, saw that both barrels were charged, then snapped it shut. Quietly, he let himself out the back door, intending to sneak down through the alley to the livery stable where he would steal a horse and be on his way.

As he walked by the rear of the buildings, he was able to recognize the saloon by the strong smell of beer and whiskey. He remembered then that this was where Dane Calder was going to wait for his money. He also saw an outside stairway going up to the second floor of the saloon, and he got an idea. With Calder thinking he was in jail, he would, like as not, have his guard down. There would never be a better time than right now.

Looking around quickly to make certain he wasn't being watched, Al started up the stairs to the second floor of the saloon.

Inside the saloon, Dane had played enough hands to determine that the men were playing an honest game. Whether their honesty was the result of their fear of him or whether they were honest men, he didn't know, but he was enjoying the game. Of course, the fact that he had won nearly fifty dollars so far helped him enjoy it. In between hands, he excused himself to step over to the bar to get another drink.

As Dane was standing at the bar watching the bartender draw his beer, he heard a sound, a soft, squeaking sound as if weight were being put down on a loose board. He glanced into the mirror and saw, at the top of the stairs, a man standing there, aiming a shotgun at him. At first the man was in shadows, but as he stepped forward Dane saw the face, plastered with an evil, victorious grin. It was Al Santos!

"Bartender, get down!" Dane shouted, spinning around and drawing his pistol at the same time.

"I'm going to kill you, Calder! You can't get away this time," Al shouted down from above. The shotgun boomed loudly.

Dane fired just as Al squeezed his own trigger. Dane had jumped to his right at almost the same time he yelled at the bartender. It was a good thing Dane had moved, because the heavy charge of buckshot from Al's gun tore a large hole in the top side of the bar, right where he had been standing. Some of the shot hit the whiskey bottles and the mirror behind the bar, and pieces of glass flew everywhere. The mirror fell except for a few jagged shards that hung in place. The shards reflected a dozen twisted images of the dramatic scene that was playing out before it.

Dane's shot had been more accurately placed than Al's, and Al dropped his weapon and grabbed his throat. He stood there, dumbly for a moment, clutching his neck as blood spilled between his fingers. Then his eyes rolled up in his head and he fell, twisting around so that, on his back and head-first, he slid down the stairs, following his clattering shotgun. He lay motionless on the bottom step with open but sightless eyes staring up toward the ceiling.

Even before the cloud of gun smoke rolled away the sheriff was coming in through the swinging doors, his hair matted with blood. He had his pistol drawn, and he stopped as he appraised the situation.

"It was self-defense, Sheriff," Broomfield said.

He pointed to Al's body. "That fella threw down on Calder with a shotgun."

"Yeah, I know," the sheriff answered. "He stole the shotgun from my office." He put his pistol away, and it wasn't until that moment that Dane put his own Colt away. "I'm sorry about that Calder. He managed to trick me. Are you all right?"

"Yeah."

The sheriff walked over and looked down at Al's body. "It's a funny thing," he said.

"What's funny?" Dane wanted to know.

"Why did he come in here?" the sheriff asked. "I mean, he got out of my jail. If he had kept on going, he would have made it. Instead, he stopped by to try and kill you. If he hadn't done that he would have been free."

"No, he wouldn't have been," Dane said easily. "I would have caught up with him again, just like I'm going to catch the others."

The sheriff looked at Dane, then shook his head. "Calder, I hope to hell you don't ever come after me for anything," he said.

"Don't get any paper out on you and I won't," Dane said.

The sheriff looked around at the other men who were, only now, crowding close to Al's body to get a good look. "How about a couple of you fellas get him down to Haller's Funeral Home," the sheriff said.

"The reward money here yet?" Dane asked.

"I'll go down to the telegraph office. The authorization should be there by now," the sheriff replied.

"I'd like to get it and be gone," Dane said. He finished his beer, then set the glass down and wiped the back of his hand across his mouth as he watched Al's body being dragged out of the saloon.

The sheriff started to leave, then he stopped and looked back at Dane.

"Look, I'm sorry about this, Calder. I should have been paying more attention to what I was doin' than to let him pull a fool stunt on me like he done."

"Yeah, well, don't worry about it," Dane replied. "But it does look to me like I could've saved us both a lot of trouble if I had just gone ahead and blown his brains out like I started to."

"Would you have really done that?"

"You play poker, Sheriff?"

"Yeah, sure."

Dane smiled. "Then you know better than to ask that question."

CHAPTER 12

"WHERE DO YOU RECKON AL IS?" GUS ASKED.

Morgan walked over to pour himself another cup of coffee and took a drink before he answered.

"I'll be damned if I know," he said.

"He said he would meet us in Brimstone," Tim said. "Why don't we just go into Brimstone and wait for him?"

"Because I don't want him wanderin' up an' down the streets of Brimstone askin' ever'body about us," Morgan replied. "If we're goin' to go in there and do a proper job at robbin' the bank, we got to go in unnoticed, hit the bank hard, and get out fast."

"You shouldn't have let him ride off by hisself," Tim said.

"Hell, I didn't really have no choice," Morgan said. "You seen how jumpy he was. I don't like bein' around anyone that jumpy. There's no tellin' what kind of trouble he could cause for us."

"Then why do we need him for the bank job in Brimstone?" Gus wanted to know.

Morgan finished his coffee, then tossed the grounds out of the cup.

"We don't," he said easily. "But I done told him about it. And since he knows where we're goin' and what we're goin' to do, I'd rather have him jumpy with us, where we can keep an eye on him, than jumpy somewhere else."

"You want me to ride back and see if I can find him anywhere?" Parish asked.

"Yes," Morgan said.

"Might take me one or two days," Parish said. "Where will I find you?"

"You know the town of Boulder Bluff?"

"Yeah, it's about ten miles this side of Brimstone," Parish said. "I know it."

"That's where we'll be waitin' for you," Morgan said. "Be there by Wednesday."

Parish pulled a piece of paper from his saddlebag and wrote, "Boulder Bluff, Wednesday."

"What's that for?"

"Just so's I don't forget," Parish said. He started saddling his horse.

"Parish?" Morgan said.

Parish didn't answer but raised his eyebrows as he looked back at Morgan.

"If you find Al in jail and there's no way you can get him out, kill him."

"What?" Tim asked. "Morgan, what do you want to do somethin' like that for?"

"You know Al as well as anybody," Morgan said. "If they start puttin' the pressure on him, how long you think he'll keep secret about our plans for Brimstone?"

Tim sighed and stroked his chin. "Not long, I reckon," he admitted.

"You want to wind up in jail, or maybe dead, because Al can't keep his mouth shut?"

"No," Tim admitted.

"All right," Morgan said. He looked at Parish. "Will you have any problems with that?"

"No," Parish answered as he swung up into his saddle. "But then, I never really cared much for the sniveling coward anyway," he added.

"Remember, be in Boulder Bluff on Wednesday," Morgan said. "You got that? Wednesday."

"Wednesday," Parish agreed. He slapped his legs against the side of his horse, and a few moments later he disappeared into the darkness.

"Morgan," Gus asked. "What happens if he don't meet us on Wednesday?"

"We'll do the job without him," Morgan said.

"But there are only three of us now."

Morgan smiled. "Well, ten thousand cut three ways is a hell of a lot better than ten thousand cut four ways," he said.

———

THE NIGHT CREATURES called to each other as Dane stood looking toward the little town of Los Pinos. A cloud passed over the moon then moved away, painting the little town before him in hues of silver and black. From here it was easy to pick out the cantina, for it was clearly the biggest and most brightly lit building in the entire town.

Dane could hear someone playing guitar. Whoever it was, was good, and the music spilled out in a steady beat with two or three poignant minor chords at the end of each phrase. A single-string melody worked its way in and out of the chords, like a thread of gold woven through the finest cloth. Dane like that kind of music. It was mournful and lonesome, the kind of melody a man could let run through his mind during the long quiet rides.

It had been four days since he killed Al, and Morgan Cottrell's trail had gone cold on him. He knew only that Cottrell and his men had been headed in this direction, and it was likely that they were either in this town now or at least had been here. And the only way to find out for sure was to go in and see.

Dane decided to hobble his horse out there in the stand of cottonwood trees. That way he could enter town without being seen.

As Dane started toward the town, he caught the smell of beans and beef coming from one of the houses and realized that he hadn't eaten all day. His stomach growled in protest, and he decided he would have himself a real café supper tonight. After first having a drink.

Dane could hear the noises of civilization as he

approached the town. A dog barked but was quickly silenced. A baby cried. A Mexican housewife raised her voice in one of the houses, rending the air with a string of invectives.

Then, as Dane entered the town, he departed from his usual pattern. Normally he would walk down the middle of the street to avoid ambush from the shadows, but this was an entirely different situation. This time the shadows, instead of being his enemy, were his ally. He moved through them, staying out of sight until he reached the cantina. There, he paused to listen to the sounds from inside. The music had stopped, and now there was only conversation. All of it seemed to be in Spanish.

Dane looked up and down the street to make certain no one was watching the cantina door, then he stepped up onto the board porch and pushed his way in. He headed for the bar, positioning himself in a way that put his back to the wall.

"Si, señor?" the bartender asked, moving over to wait on him.

"Do you have beer?"

"No, señor. Only tequila."

"That'll do," Dane said, slapping a coin on the bar. His pocket was full of more money now than it had been for a while. He had won fifty dollars in the poker game, and he had the two-hundred-dollar reward that was paid for Al Santos.

At the opposite end of the bar stood a tall, bearded man. Watching himself in the mirror, the bearded man tossed his drink down and wiped the back of his hand across his mouth. Then he turned to look at Dane.

"Hey, you."

Dane did not respond.

"I'm talkin' to you, mister, the fella at the end of the bar."

Dane looked at the man but still said nothing.

"Ain't you Dane Calder?"

Dane didn't answer.

"That is you, ain't it?" the man persisted. "A big ugly bastard. I seen you once in Thunder Ridge."

By now the other people in the bar, even those who didn't speak English that well, could recognize the escalating challenge, and they began to move out of the way. Like a macabre ballet, the intricate dance of death had already begun.

"Morgan Cottrell send you to do his dirty work?" Dane asked. It was his first response.

"Morgan Cottrell? No, I don't know nothin' 'bout Morgan Cottrell. This here is between me and you."

Dane was puzzled. As far as he knew, he had never seen the man before.

"Have we got a beef, mister?" Dane asked.

"Yeah, we got a beef," the man replied. "The name is Marshall. You ever hear of me? Syl Marshall?"

"Can't say as I have."

"Well now, that's the beef I got, you see," Marshall said. "Ever'one's heard of the great Dane Calder. But no one's ever heard of Syl Marshall. But

I think they'll know me after today." He laughed. "Yes, sir, after today I'll be known as the man who killed Dane Calder."

Dane pinched the bridge of his nose and closed his eyes. It wasn't enough that he had to fight men like Morgan Cottrell and the killers Cottrell sent after him. There were also too many times like this where he encountered someone who was trying to make a name for himself. He didn't like these incidents. In the first place, they were dangerous because they were unexpected and anything could happen. In the second place, he thought it was a waste of time and effort to kill someone unless it was in the line of business. And yet, here he was, in a foul-smelling cantina in a little town he had never been before, having to face the situation yet one more time.

Dane put his glass down with a tired sigh and turned to face Marshall.

"Marshall, you don't really want to do this, do you?" he hissed. It was more than a question. It was a threat.

Marshall stepped away from the bar and flipped his coat back so that the handle of his pistol was exposed.

"Yeah," he said defiantly. "Yeah, I do wanna do it."

Dane studied the man's eyes. Having been in this situation so many times before, he knew that the eyes never lied. They told him how frightened or confident his adversary was, where he was going to shoot, and more importantly, when he was going to make his first move.

Marshall made his move, though Dane had read it in his eyes quickly enough so that his own gun came out at almost the same time. The cantina was shattered with the roar of two pistols exploding. The others yelled and dived for cover as white gun smoke billowed out in a cloud that filled the center of the room, momentarily obscuring everything.

As the smoke began to clear, Marshall stared through the white cloud, smiling broadly at Dane. He opened his mouth as if to speak, but the only sound he could make was a gagging rattle, way back in his throat. The smile left his face, his eyes glazed over, and he pitched forward, his gun clattering to the floor.

Dane stood ready to fire a second shot if necessary, but it wasn't. His first bullet had gone right through Marshall's heart.

"*Ole!*" someone shouted, and the guitar player began strumming a fast, joyful tune. Nearly everyone else in the cantina began laughing and singing and dancing around gaily. It was the most bizarre reaction to a shooting Dane had ever seen, and he stood there, looking at the celebration in surprise.

"You are wondering why there is so much happiness, no?" the bartender asked, pouring Dane another tequila, even though he hadn't asked for it.

"It does seem a little strange," Dane agreed.

"It is because Señor Marshall is dead," the

bartender said. "Señor Marshall was a very evil man. You have made us all free, señor, and now the town is yours."

"I don't want the town," Dane said. "All I want is something to eat and a place to sleep."

At the other end of the bar, Dane noticed a young boy, perhaps twelve years old, sweeping the floor.

"You, boy," Dane called, pulling out a few more coins. "You know the stand of cottonwood trees just south of town?"

"Si," the boy answered.

Dane tossed the money to him. "You'll find my horse there. Bring him into town and put him up in the livery."

The boy took the money and scooted out the front door.

"There a hotel in this town?"

"Next door," the bartender answered.

"When the boy gets back with my horse, tell him where I am."

"Si, señor," the bartender said.

There was a café in the front of the hotel, and Dane ordered a meal of steak and eggs. The boy came in before he was finished eating.

"I put up your horse, señor."

"Gracias," Dane said. "You want to eat supper?"

"I do not have money for a fine supper," the boy answered.

Dane signaled to the waitress to bring another order of steak and eggs. A moment later, as the boy chewed thoughtfully on a piece of steak, he looked at Dane.

"In the cantina, the people are celebrating," the boy said. "Soon, I think, there will be a great festival to honor you. You are a hero, Señor Calder."

"Who was this man, Marshall?"

"He was the *alguacil*, señor. The sheriff," the boy explained.

"The sheriff?" Dane asked, looking up in surprise. "How did the town ever choose such a man for their sheriff?"

"He was not elected to be sheriff, señor. He was not even hired for the job. He became the sheriff because he killed the old one and took his badge. He made everyone in town pay him much money to keep away the evil, but he was the most evil of them all." The boy smiled. "Now, you can be the sheriff."

"Seems to me that's how the town got into trouble in the first place," Dane said.

"Si. But you are not like Señor Marshall."

"How do you know?"

"I can tell, señor," the boy insisted.

"Maybe not. But I didn't kill Marshall to become the sheriff of this town," Dane said. "I killed him because he was trying to kill me."

"Si, but it does not matter why you killed him," the boy explained. "It only matters *that* you killed him."

"Yeah, well, you tell the people in this town to get their own sheriff. I am not interested."

"Maybe you will not be the sheriff," the boy said.

"But you are still the hero. And because I am sharing your dinner with you, many will think I am your friend and I will be a hero too."

Dane smiled. "Well you are my amigo," he agreed. "But as for being a hero...well, take my word for it. That isn't all it's cracked up to be."

CHAPTER 13

ALTHOUGH IT WAS NEARLY MIDNIGHT, THEY WERE still celebrating when Parish stopped at the cantina for a drink. Sent by Morgan to find out what was keeping Al, Parish had learned of Al's shootout with Calder and was now on his way back to make the report. He stopped in San Ingacio, not because he knew that Calder was in town, but because he wanted a drink. He learned about Calder only because the bartender was anxious to talk.

"It happened right here, señor, in this very cantina," the bartender said. "A fight between two *pistoleros*—Syl Marshall, a very evil man, and Señor Calder. Señor Calder killed Marshall and is now our deliverer."

"What's that? Calder was here, in this town?" Parish asked.

"He was. A big man who is known as *the* bounty hunter," the bartender said.

"That's him, all right," Parish said. "How long ago did he leave town?"

"Oh, he has not left town, señor. We are much honored for he is here, staying at the hotel in this very village. Señor Calder. Is he your *amigo*?"

"*Si*," Parish answered. "He is my *amigo*."

"You must be a good man to have an *amigo* like Señor Dane Calder," the bartender said. "Have another drink, señor. It will cost you nothing."

"Really?" Parish said, smiling broadly. He held the glass out, then laughed. "Well now, that's a pretty good joke on old Calder," he said. "Yes, sir, that's a pretty good joke."

The hotel clerk was an American, and from the way he looked at Dane he may have been a friend or at least a business associate of Syl Marshall's.

"It's room 202," the clerk said coldly. "Upstairs and all the way to the back. The last door on the right."

"Thanks," Dane said, signing the registration book.

"Checkout time is eight o'clock in the morning," the clerk added.

"Isn't that a little early?"

"It is our procedure," the clerk said.

"Yeah, well, I'll be gone before that," Dane assured him. He draped his saddlebags over his right shoulder and, carrying his rifle in his left, climbed the stairs to the second floor where he came upon a long hallway. The hall carpet was maroon with a floral design. The wallpaper was a cream color with dark blue stripes. Kerosene lanterns were mounted on gimbals on the wall beside every door, and all were burning brightly so that the hall itself was well lighted. The hall was L-shaped with three rooms on each side, then a sharp turn to the left. Room 202 was the last door on the right. At the end of the hall was a window that faced the street.

Dane extinguished the lantern nearest the window so he could stand in the shadow and look outside. He stood to one side of the window and peered cautiously through the curtain. Even though it was dark outside, there was enough light from the moon and from the lights of the saloon to see out onto the street. He saw the shadows of a couple of men sitting on the porch of the apothecary across the street. They were smoking cigarettes, and once he saw the soft gleam of a bottle being passed between them. Then, when one of them turned his head, Dane saw the sombrero, and he knew that they represented no danger to him.

Dane unlocked the door to his room and checked inside. It was a typical hotel room, consisting of a bed, a washstand, and a lamp table. There were two open windows in the room, and a gentle cross breeze filled the muslin curtains which hung over them. Dane took off his holster and boots, slipped his pistol under his pillow, then lay down. He was asleep in less than five minutes.

———

SIMON PARISH SAT at a table near the wall of the cantina, nursing his drink and watching the others. He knew that Dane Calder was there, in this very town, right now. What he didn't know was what he should do about it. Should he go back and tell the others, or should he take care of it himself?

Hell, he thought. How could he take care of it himself? Look how many men had tried, and how many of them had failed. Still, this seemed like too good an opportunity to pass up.

A man approached his table, and when Parish looked up, he saw that it was another American.

"Mind if I share your table, friend?" the American asked. He pointed to the others. "I get a little tired of bein' surrounded by Mexicans all the time."

"Yeah, I know what you mean," Parish replied. He held up his glass. "This is tequila. A man can't even get a decent drink here," he added. "Don't know how an American can live here."

"Are you kiddin'?" the stranger asked. "Americans have it made here. That is, we did have, and if things work out right, we will again. By the way, the name's Palmer. Chris Palmer."

"Simon Parish."

"You're on a dodger, ain't you, Parish? It's a new one, just come out, but it is you, ain't it?"

Parish's eyes narrowed, and he stared at Palmer. "That's not a very polite question to ask a man, Palmer," he said coldly. "Not a very safe one, either."

Palmer chuckled and held out his hand.

"Nothin' for you to be concerned about," he said quickly. "I ain't the law, and I sure as hell ain't no bounty hunter."

"Then why did you bring it up?"

"Because Dane Calder is a bounty hunter," Palmer said.

"Yes, I guess he is."

"And he is here, in this village, right over there in the hotel," Palmer went on.

Parish raised his glass and took a swallow, studying Palmer over the rim.

"That's what the bartender told me," he said. "But what makes you think I'm interested?"

Palmer chuckled. "Oh, I know you're interested, Mister Parish, because you been askin' questions about him," he said.

"What if I have?"

"He's on your trail, ain't he?"

"Could be. But if he is, what business is that of yours? Especially if, as you say, you ain't the law and you ain't a bounty hunter."

"Parish, I think maybe you and me could do a little business together," Palmer suggested. "That is, if you're game."

"What's the business?"

"You know how I know'd there was a dodger on you? Because I seen it over at the sheriff's office. I am the deputy sheriff in this town."

Parish drew back from him. "I thought you said you wasn't the law."

Palmer chuckled. "Well, I ain't the kind of law

you got to worry about, if you know what I mean. You see, Marshall was the sheriff, and him and me had sort of an arrangement worked out with this town."

"The fella everyone is celebratin' his dyin'? That's the sheriff you were deputy to?" Parish asked.

"Yep," Palmer answered. "And you better believe it was one sweet deal. Me and Marshall was bleedin' these Mexicans white. They was payin' taxes for this and taxes for that; ever'time we could think up a new one, we would slap another tax on 'em."

"And they paid?"

"Just like sheep, Parish, just like sheep," he said. "Also, we had a sweet deal with outlaws on the run," he added. "They paid Marshall a little tax of their own, and they could stay here, in town, have a few drinks, eat some real food, and lay up over at the brothels, all without fear of being caught."

"It sounds like you had quite an operation here," Parish said.

"We did. And we can again," Palmer said. "But first, we're goin' to have to get rid of Mr. Calder."

"Why? Hell, he'll be gone tomorrow or the next day. If you know anything about him, you know that he never stays long, anywhere."

"Just goin' away won't do it," Palmer said. "You see, with Marshall dead, the Mexicans and the Americans who weren't in on Marshall's deal are already talkin' about havin' a real election, to get a real sheriff. I'm afraid that by killin' Marshall like he done, Calder has given these people a little backbone that they never had before."

"Well, what's done is done. I guess there's nothin' you can do about that."

"Oh, but there is, Mr. Parish," Palmer said, smiling broadly. "You see, if someone was to kill Dane Calder, I figure all the backbone would be taken out of these people. If they see that even a man like Calder can get hisself killed, they'll think twice before tryin' anything on their own. I can declare myself the new sheriff, and we'll be right back where we were." Palmer's smile broadened. "Only, it'll be even better for me, 'cause I won't have Marshall around to share it with."

"So, what are you sayin', Palmer? You're plannin' on killin' Dane Calder?"

"Yes, but not alone," Palmer answered. "Unless I miss my guess, Parish, you want him dead just as much as I do. And if you don't, you should, 'cause believe me, he will find you."

"All right, suppose I do want him dead? You got any ideas how to go about it? Because I don't mind tellin' you, Palmer, some friends and I have been tryin' to kill Calder for the last two or three weeks. Dane Calder is a man that takes a heap of killin'."

"Yeah, well, maybe he'd kill easier if we did it while he was in bed," Palmer suggested. He pointed in the direction of the hotel. "He's over there, right now, sound asleep."

"How are we going to get to him without the desk clerk giving the alarm?" Parish asked.

Palmer laughed out loud.

"That's a good one," he said.

"What do you mean?"

"The desk clerk is my brother," Palmer explained. "When I get control of this town, *he* has control."

Parish reached across the table and shook Palmer's hand.

"Palmer," he said, "if you want the bastard dead, you got yourself a partner."

———

DANE WAS DREAMING that he was back with the Apaches. The sun was low and the range was fire-red in its glow. Dane had never seen such red. It blazed up at him with the deep crimson of blood. The earth was spread with blood.

"Señor!"

The warning cry cut through the layers of sleep as quickly as a knife through hot butter. The dream fell away, and Dane, with reflexes born of years of living on the edge, rolled off the bed just as a gun boomed in the doorway of his room. The bullet slammed into the headboard of the bed where, a second earlier, Dane had been sleeping.

At the same time Dane rolled off the bed, he grabbed the pistol from under his pillow. Now the advantage was his. The man who had attempted to kill him was temporarily blinded by the muzzle flash of his own shot and he could see nothing in the darkness of Dane's room. That same muzzle flash, however, had illuminated the assailant for Dane, and he quickly aimed his pistol at the dark hulk in the doorway, closed his eyes against his own muzzle flash, and squeezed the trigger. The gun bucked in his hand as the roar filled the room.

To Dane, there was a measurable amount of time between the explosion of the intruder's gun and his own. To other patrons of the hotel, or those in the nearby buildings, however, the two shots came so close together as to be almost simultaneous. In a little village like Los Pinos, drunken patrons of the cantina often vented their spirits with the discharge of pistols. But the villagers had learned to recognize the difference in the sound of shots fired in play and those fired in anger. Everyone within hearing knew that these were angry shots.

Dane heard a groaning sound, then the heavy thump of a falling body.

"Señor? Señor, are you hurt?" the Mexican boy asked in a quiet voice.

"No," Dane said. "I'm all right." He moved through the door and out into the hallway, stepping over the body of the man he had just shot. There was the snapping of a powder cap, then the boom of a cartridge as another shot was fired, this one from the elbow where the hallway veered left. The fire flash lit up the hallway, and in the quick wink of its flare, Dane recognized Simon Parish. Dane shot back, and his bullet shattered the glass globe of the lantern near the corner, but by the time Dane's own muzzle flash had died down, Parish was gone.

Dane hurried down to the end of the hallway and searched, noticing for the first time that the hallway was no longer brightly lit. Not only the lantern he had extinguished, but all the others were out as well. As a result, the hallway was very dark, and in that darkness he could see nothing.

"Señor!" the Mexican boy called. "Señor," he called again, and this time Dane recognized urgency in the boy's voice.

Dane hurried back down the hall and found the boy crouched low, behind the bed.

"I am all right, señor," the boy said with a tense smile. "The man missed me, and I hid. I did not want to die."

Relief washed over Dane, and he clapped the boy on the shoulder. "You did well, kid. You're a quick thinker. What's your name?"

"I am Pablo, your amigo," he said as a wide smile crossed his face.

"You are indeed. How did you know to warn me?"

"I hear Señor Palmer talking to another man in the saloon. He say he wants to kill you so he can be new sheriff in Los Pinos."

"Who is Palmer?" Dane asked.

Pablo pointed to the dead body. "That is Señor Palmer. He was a man of much evil, like Señor Marshall. I do not know who the other man was."

"I know who he was. He is one of the men I am searching for, but I didn't know he was in this town."

"Maybe he is still here. Maybe he go back to the saloon," Pablo said. "I can go see."

Dane walked over to the window and looked outside. At the far end of town he saw the shadow of a man riding fast, and he knew it had to be Parish.

"No need, Pablo," Dane said. "But I know which way to head out in the morning."

CHAPTER 14

THOUGH HE HAD PAID FOR THE ROOM FOR AN ENTIRE night, after the excitement, Dane was ready to leave town, so he left shortly after midnight. It was midmorning now, and the sun was halfway up to noon.

Ahead of him the sunburned land lay in empty folds of rocks, hot, yellow sand, and prickly cactus. Undulating waves rose up from the sun-heated ground, causing those objects close by to shimmer, and forming ghost lakes to lie tantalizingly in the distance.

Parish's horse went lame. Dane picked it up immediately by the gait of the animal and the slight dragging of one foot. He also knew that it wasn't something simple, like a loose shoe or even a stone bruise. This was serious. The horse would probably have to be destroyed.

Almost as soon as Dane came to that conclusion, he heard the shot. It was a distant echo, short and flat, rolling across the plains. From the sound of it, Dane knew that his quarry was at least two or three miles distant. And he was now on foot. No chance now that he would lead Dane to the others.

It was ten or twelve minutes before Dane reached the dead animal. He saw that Parish hadn't even bothered to remove the saddle, not wanting to be burdened with it in his hasty flight. He followed Parish's boot prints off to the southwest. Figuring that a horse covered ground about twice as fast as a man, he calculated that he was no more than five or six minutes behind Parish now. He started after the tracks.

Dane was following a narrow ridge when he heard the shot. It was followed by a woman's scream, then another shot. Dane kicked his horse into a gallop and within a few moments crested a little hill. He saw in front of him a buckboard and a man and woman. The man was lying on the ground; the woman was sitting with him, cradling the man's head in her lap. The traces of the buckboard were empty.

As Dane approached, the woman looked up and began to scream again.

"Hold it, lady, hold it," Dane said, holding his hand out toward her. "I'm not going to hurt you."

"My—my husband," the woman said. "He's been shot. Help him. Please, help him."

Dane swung down from his horse and looked at the man. It didn't take but one quick glance to see that the man was dead.

"Ma'am," he said quietly.

"He's—he's dead, isn't he?" she asked.

"Yes, ma'am. I'm afraid he is," Dane said.

The woman began sobbing then and Dane stood there for a moment, not sure what he should do next. Then he noticed that there was blood on the woman's dress, a lot of blood, more blood than could be accounted for by her husband's wound.

"Miss?" Dane asked. "Are you shot?"

"I-I don't know," the woman said. She looked down at her lap, and then over at her leg. "Yes," she said. "Yes, I must be. That's funny…I don't remember, I just—I just…" The woman's eyelids fluttered, then closed, and she fell back in a dead faint.

Dane sighed. He had to hand it to Parish. It was an act of genius, evil genius to be sure, but genius, nevertheless. He had killed the man and wounded the woman. If he had killed both the man and the woman, Dane could have stayed on his trail. But by leaving the woman alive and wounded, he had given Dane no choice but to look after her.

It was about five miles back to the man and woman's ranch. He found their place by back tracking the trail that was left by the buckboard wheels. Dane's horse wasn't broken to the trace, and he fought and fidgeted all the way. It wasn't a very easy trip, but eventually they made it back.

Dane took the woman inside and laid her on the bed. This was the first time he was able to get a good look at her, and he saw that she was actually quite pretty. She had light brown hair and blue eyes. She was a young woman.

The pain of being moved and the shock of what she was going through kept the woman unconscious most of the time, and for that Dane was glad. Now he was going to have to find the wound.

Dane cut the bottom half of the woman's dress off, then the petticoat, and finally the bottom part of her knee-length bloomers, though he did leave enough of the bloomers to preserve some modicum of modesty. The bullet hole was in her left thigh, about eight inches above the knee. It was black and ugly, but the entry was fairly clean and he believed he could remove the bullet without too much difficulty…if she would let him.

He got some water and began bathing her face with a cloth until finally she came to.

She looked at him for a moment as if questioning with her eyes who he was. Then she remembered what had happened and raised her hand to her mouth. Her eyes flooded with tears. "My husband?" she asked.

"I'm sorry," Dane said. "He's out in the buckboard."

"He's dead, isn't he?"

"Yes, ma'am."

"And I've been shot?"

"Yes, ma'am."

"Am I dying?"

"No, ma'am," Dane was glad to able to say. "But

the bullet's going to have to come out. I can do it if you'll let me."

"Yes, of course, I'll let you," the woman said. "Why wouldn't I?"

"Well, for one thing, it's going to hurt."

"I have given birth," the woman said. "I can take pain."

"Also, it is in a rather delicate spot," Dane went on. "It's in your left leg…very high up on your leg."

The woman began feeling her leg with her hand and noticed then, for the first time, that her legs were bare. She looked up at Dane with questioning eyes.

"I'm sorry," Dane said. "I had to find the wound."

"Yes." She sighed. "Well, you've found it, so how much more delicate can it be? Go ahead, take it out."

"I'll need to get a fire started," Dane said.

"There's firewood in the box, matches just above the stove."

"You said you gave birth," Dane said as he gathered the sticks of firewood. He glanced around the house for any signs of a child.

"Yes," she said. "A girl. She died last winter."

"I'm sorry," Dane said. He saw a bottle of whiskey. "Uh, ma'am, I don't want to offend you, but it would help if you could drink a little whiskey. I know you don't normally, but—"

Dane was interrupted by the woman's laugh. "I used to drink whiskey for a living. Now, my name is

Mattie Wade. Frank Wade took me away from that old life."

"He must have been a good man," Dane said.

"He was. He brought me here and we've had a good life together."

"How much of that can you drink?" Dane asked as he handed her the bottle.

"I gave up the sportin' life. I didn't give up my taste for liquor. How about if I just finish off the bottle?"

Dane smiled. "That would be good," he said.

Dane got the fire started in the stove while Mattie finished the bottle. Then, when she was good and drunk and the stove was roaring hot, he put a poker in the flames, heated up his knife, and walked over to look down at her.

"Are you ready?" he asked.

She took a deep breath, then let out a long sigh. "I guess I'm as ready as I'll ever be," she said.

Dane gave her a rolled-up cloth. "Here," he said. "Bite on this."

———

DANE TOOK a pan of biscuits from the oven, then checked on the bacon. In another pan he was frying potatoes, and as the bacon came out, he stirred in some flour to make gravy. Behind him, he heard Mattie groan. He set the skillet aside to keep from burning anything, then walked over to the bed.

"Good morning," he said.

"I slept through the whole night?" she asked.

"You were in and out, but mostly out. How do you feel?"

"My leg hurts," she said.

"I'm sure it does, but it isn't festering," Dane said. "How's your head?"

"My head?" She put her hand to her head. "Now that you ask, it does hurt."

"I shouldn't wonder," Dane said. "You drank enough last night."

"A hangover? Oh, my, I haven't had a hangover in over two years." She smiled. "What you're cookin' smells good."

"That's a good sign," Dane said. "If you can want foot, even with a hangover, then your leg has to be healing up just fine."

"Yes, well, I am hungry," Mattie said. She sat up and swung her legs over the edge of the bed, then looked at the bandage. "You did a pretty good job of bandaging," she noted.

"I've patched a few bullet and knife wounds in my time," Dane said.

"Are you a lawman?" Mattie asked. "You didn't tell me your name."

"Dane Calder, and no, I am not a lawman."

"Dane Calder, the bounty hunter," Mattie said. "I guess you have taken care of a few bullet holes before."

Dane did not answer as he continued getting the food ready.

"I'd like to eat at the table if I can," she said.

"Sure," Dane agreed. He helped her up, but she was able to walk to the table by herself.

"What did you do with Frank?" she asked.

"I found your little girl's grave," Dane said. "I put Frank beside her."

Mattie was silent for a long moment, and though her eyes teared again, she didn't cry. "Thanks," she finally said. "He'll like it there."

Dane brought the food over from the stove and they began to eat.

"The man who shot Frank and stole our horse," Mattie said. "He was running from you, wasn't he?"

"Yes."

"Who is he?"

"His name is Parish, Simon Parish. He's part of Morgan Cottrell's gang."

"What is he wanted for?" Mattie asked.

"Bank robbery, jailbreaking, and now, murder," Dane said.

"Are you going to catch him?"

"Oh, yes, I'll catch him," Dane said.

Mattie chewed thoughtfully for a moment, then she said, "Not if you hang around here any longer."

"I was going to talk to you about that," Dane said.

"Go," she ordered. "Go now. I want you to find that bastard, and I want you to shoot him dead. And when you do, I want you to take just a moment to think of Frank."

————

"YOU MISERABLE PIECE OF HORSEFLESH," Parish said,
hitting the horse with a length of trace line. When
Parish took him, the horse had been attached to a
buckboard, so there was no saddle. To add to his
troubles the halter and harness were not designed
for riding. On top of that, the horse was not used to
being ridden, and though he didn't buck Parish off,
he was balky and hard to handle. Sometimes, like
now, he would stop, and no amount of urging would
make him go again. At such times, Parish would
have to get off and lead him by the halter for several
minutes before he could get back on. As a result,
though he had not even stopped to sleep, he had
covered barely ten miles during the night.

"Let's go," Parish said, slapping his legs against
the side of the horse.

The horse just stood there.

"All right, all right!" Parish said angrily. He
jumped down, then walked around in front of the
horse and grabbed hold of the animal's halter. He
began walking, and obediently the horse walked
along with him.

"I tell you what I should've done," he said,
speaking to the horse as if the horse could understand him. "I should have taken the buckboard. If I
had, I'd be a hell of a lot farther along than I am
now."

Parish sighed and ran his hand through his hair.

"No," he said. "No, what I should've done is kill
Dane Calder."

After several more minutes, Parish was able to

mount the horse again. Then, just after remounting, he heard the unmistakable and very welcome sound of a train whistle.

"A train whistle!" he said. "There's a train up ahead!"

Parish began slapping his legs against the animal's side, urging him on, trying to get him to break into a gallop, but all he could get was a slight increase in the rate of walking. When he crested the next ridge, he saw the train sitting by a water tower. The train was heading east. That was the wrong direction; he needed to go west to rejoin Morgan and the others. He thought about it for a second, then decided that it didn't really matter. The most important thing to him now was to get away from Dane Calder, and this was just the way it could be done.

"Hurry up, horse," he demanded, kicking the animal as hard as he could in the sides. "If you don't get me there in time to catch the train, I'm going to blow your brains out."

CHAPTER 15

BY THE TIME DANE REACHED THE RAILROAD TRACK the train had already left. There was no doubt in his mind that Parish was on the train, for Dane found the Wade horse tied to one of the legs of the water tower. A pencil-thin line of smoke on the distant horizon marked where the train had been.

Dane turned the Wade horse loose, gave it a swat, and was glad to see that it had started back for the ranch. Mattie would need her horse.

Dane gave his own horse water, then took off his bedroll, long gun, and saddlebags, making the load as light as possible. There was still a chance to catch the train if he was lucky. Of course, he wouldn't be able to catch up to it by chasing directly after it, but there was a way.

Dane knew that just east of here were several deep ravines and spine-back ridges. The railroad company, in its wisdom, had decided that it would be cheaper and easier to route the track around the badlands than to build the system of bridge and trestles required to go straight across. As a result, the track bowed south, making a great, wide loop and using well over twenty miles of track while actually only advancing a little over one mile farther to the west.

The ravines and gullies weren't easy for a horse to negotiate either, but they could be crossed, and if Dane could do it quickly enough, he could be on the other side of them by the time the train finished its transit of the oxbow.

Hiding his jettisoned equipment, Dane tightened the cinch on his saddle, then started out. He pushed his horse into a ground-eating lope and was at the western edge of the badlands in just a few minutes.

There was no ground-eating lope in crossing the badlands though. In fact, Dane was lucky when he could even ride, for there were many times he would have to get off and lead his horse. It was hot, exhausting work, climbing up out of one gully, only to find another one no more than one hundred yards in front of him. But Dane pressed on.

When Dane reached the far side of the gullies, he heard the distant whistle of the train and realized that he wasn't going to make it through in time. He cursed once in frustration, then saw something that might mean success after all.

As the train came out of its oxbow, it would pass through a long, twisting cut between the steep walls of two high buttes. Dane was just on the opposite side of one of those buttes now. If he could climb it quickly enough, then go down the other side, he could, perhaps, get to the track before the train arrived. There was no way for his horse to go over of course, and actually Dane wasn't sure he could even do it himself.

But he was damned sure going to try.

———

ON BOARD the train at that very moment, Parish was sitting at a window seat looking at the brown-and-yellow landscape as it whipped by outside. A little wisp of train smoke drifted by the window, and Parish looked ahead to see that they were going around a long curve, thus allowing him to see the engine. The driver wheels were pounding against the track, partially obscured by the white puffs of steam that feathered out from the pistons. Parish had no idea how fast they were going, but he was sure it had to be faster than a horse could gallop.

The conductor passed down the aisle then, moving importantly from part of the train to the other.

"Conductor?"

The conductor paused at Parish's call.

"How fast would you say we was goin' right now?"

The conductor took out his pocket watch and looked at it for a few seconds, then snapped the cover closed and put it back in his pocket.

"Right now we are doing just under twenty miles per hour," he said.

"Twenty miles an hour? Can a horse go that fast?"

"Well, a racehorse can run a mile in two minutes, and that's thirty miles per hour," the conductor admitted. "But only a few horses can run that fast and they can maintain such a speed only for a short time. On the other hand, we can keep this speed up all day long," he added, smiling broadly. "Don't forget, it is possible now for a person to cross the entire United States in no more than a week, by using the railroad. Time was, not too long ago, when such a trip would take up to six months. We live in a wonderful time, my friend. Yes, sir, a wonderful time indeed."

After the conductor left, Parish stared out the window again, trying unsuccessfully to get a look behind the train. It bothered him that the conductor admitted a horse could run this fast, even if it was for just a short distance.

Parish leaned back in his seat.

Wait a minute, he told himself. Now, suppose a horse could run this fast? First of all, he had a big head start on Calder. When he got on the train, Dane Calder wasn't even in sight yet. So even if Calder's horse could run just as fast as the train, that wouldn't mean anything. He would have to run *faster* in order to catch up with him, as fast as a race-horse. And even if Calder's horse could run that fast, it couldn't keep up such a pace for very long.

There was no way Calder could catch him on this train.

Parish allowed himself a little smile. Then he remembered how many times before Calder had demonstrated how easily all logic could be defied. By all logic, Dane Calder should be dead now. And yet Dane Calder, very obviously, wasn't dead. Dane Calder was coming after him.

Parish's confidence and sense of well-being faded, and he leaned toward the window again, trying once more to look to the rear of the train. He didn't see anything, but if he had seen a horse, doggedly galloping after them, he wouldn't have been in the least bit surprised.

Parish looked around the train car at the other passengers. There were six other men, three women, and three children. Some were sleeping, a couple were reading, and a few were just looking out the window.

You fools! Parish wanted to shout at them. *Don't you realize he's coming after us? Don't you know he's back there, right now?*

He wanted to yell the words, but he said nothing. Instead, he licked his lips nervously, then pulled the pistol from his holster and checked the loads. Let *the* bounty hunter come. He was ready for him.

———

IT WAS VERY HARD GOING. Dane had been at it for a half hour and he could still see his horse, just standing there below him. Dane was now clinging to the side of the cliff, moving only when he could find the tiniest handhold, the smallest crevice for his foot. Behind him was nothing but air, and if he missed a handhold or foothold, he would drop over one hundred feet to the rocks below.

Sweat was pouring into his eyes, but he couldn't let go long enough to wipe his face.

Dane had just about reached an impasse, and he was wondering if it wouldn't be better to turn around and go back. He had climbed more than half way up, but for the last few minutes he had been unable to go on because he couldn't find another foothold.

Reluctantly, he decided to start back down. He would have to let Parish get away while he went after the others. It wasn't something he wanted to do. He felt a special obligation to get Parish now, but there was nothing he could do about it. If he went on, he could fall to his death on the rocks below, and that would accomplish nothing.

Dane reached for the handhold he had surrendered a few moments earlier, the first step in retracing his path. He got a good grip, then he moved his foot across. This time the small slate outcropping that had supported his weight earlier failed, and with a sickening sensation in his stomach, Dane felt himself falling.

He threw himself against the side, scraping and tearing at his flesh. He flailed against the wall with his hands, and after a drop of some fifteen feet, found a sturdy juniper tree. The tree supported his weight, and he hung there for a moment, looking down between his feet at the gully floor. He saw the slate outcropping that had broken under his weight hit the floor and shatter far below him.

Dane looked to his right. About four feet away from him was a narrow shelf. If he could gain that shelf he would be all right. He took a deep breath, then swung his foot to the right and up. He caught the ledge with the heel of his boot, then slowly he worked himself up, pushing away from the juniper tree until his knees were also on the ledge. Finally, he let go of the tree and worked himself up slowly until, at last, he was on the ledge.

After that it got easy. The ledge showed signs of having been a trail at one time, possibly an Indian trail that had existed until erosion took part of it away. Dane found that he could even walk upright. After a moment he was strolling as easily up the trail as if he were walking down the board sidewalks of a town. A few moments later he saw the railroad tracks and, in the distance, the approaching train. Smiling, he crawled out onto the edge of a rocky ledge and waited. Then, when the train passed underneath, he jumped down onto the top of the mail car, which was the first car just behind the tender. He squatted quickly to maintain his balance.

Although the train hadn't looked as if it were going so fast as it approached, from up here on top of the car, the ground seemed to be whipping by at a dizzying speed, and he realized this was as fast as a galloping horse. There was also a pendulum effect in the sway of the train, with the wheels being the attaching point, and the top of the car being the outer end of the pendulum arm. That meant that up here, the swaying of the car was so pronounced that it was difficult just to keep from falling off. Dane stayed on his hands and knees for a moment until he was sure of his balance, then he took a deep breath, stood up and started walking toward the rear of the train.

———

"MAMA! There's someone on top of the train," a little girl in Parish's car said. Parish's car was the first car behind the mail car.

"Hush dear," the little girl's mother said.

"But I saw him," the little girl insisted. "I saw his shadow. He was walking toward the back of the train on top of the car. He was all bent over."

"We'll ask the conductor," the little girl's mother suggested, and, as the conductor passed through the car, she summoned him.

"A man, on top of the car?" the conductor replied. He chuckled. "I wouldn't think so."

"But I saw his shadow on the ground," the little girl insisted.

The conductor moved over to the window and looked outside for a moment, then he laughed again. "Look," he said, pointing to the ground outside.

"There's a man and there's another. And that one looks like a bear, don't you think?"

"What is it?" the little girl's mother asked.

"It's the shadows," the conductor explained. "You see, as we pass through these cuts, there are many rocks of strange formations, and they cast their shadows upon the ground. Those shadows, combined with the speed at which we are moving, sometimes gives the most startling illusions. I once had a passenger insist that there was a horse on top of the train. A horse, mind you."

"Oh," the little girl's mother said. "Oh, how foolish you must think we are."

"Not at all, madam," the conductor replied with a polite touch to the bill of his cap. "As I say, it happens all the time. Please, don't feel in the least embarrassed about it."

"Mama, it wasn't a shadow," the little girl insisted, as the conductor passed on through the car.

"Hush, dear. You've caused enough of a scene as it is," her mother scolded gently.

Parish was fighting hard to hold down the bile of fear that had risen in his throat. He believed the little girl. Not only that, but if the conductor had asked him, he could give the shadow a name. He knew, just as certain as he knew his own name, that there *was* a man on top of the train, and that man could only be Dane Calder.

Well, he wasn't going to stay inside, just sitting in his seat, waiting for Calder to come. No, sir. He was going to go after him.

Parish got up and walked to the front end of the car, then, reaching the platform, looked up. Taking a deep breath, he climbed to the top of the train.

About two cars behind him, Parish saw a man rise up and run toward the rear of the train. It was Calder.

Calder had his back to Parish and didn't see him. Parish climbed over the top channel of the roof of the car to put some sort of shield between himself and Calder, then he lay down, took careful aim and fired.

Dane felt rather than heard the bullet whiz by his ear, and startled, he turned to see Parish just as he fired a second time. Quickly, Dane dropped to the roof of the car and fired back, missing Parish but seeing his bullet send out a shower of sparks as it disintegrated against the boiler-plate steel that made up the rear of the tender.

Parish fired again, missing again. Dane fired back, sending three quick shots at Parish, this time spraying him with splinters, but because he was shielded by the roof channel, doing no further damage.

Because of the noise of the train itself, no one on board the train could hear the firing and were thus unaware of the drama being played out above them.

As the train started around the curve, it exposed Parish's position behind the roof channel just enough for Dane to take a well-aimed shot. But when Dane pulled the trigger, he had a misfire. Frustrated, Dane pulled the trigger a second time, but with the same result. He had only two rounds remaining in his pistol, and both of them had misfired.

Parish realized at once that Dane was out of bullets. He stood up and ran down the cars toward Dane, holding his pistol extended in front of him, reaching him before Dane had the opportunity to reload.

"I've been waitin' a long time for this," Parish said. "You've been one hard bastard to kill, but now I'm goin' to do it."

Parish raised his pistol.

Dane saw then that the train was about to pass under the small hard-rock tunnel that marked the exit of the long, narrow draw. As Parish was standing, facing the rear of the train, he was unaware of it. "Say your prayers, Calder!" he said with an evil smile.

The train was almost to the tunnel now. The noise of the engine was passing under it, and there were only a couple of seconds left.

"Look out behind you!" Dane called, suddenly dropping flat on his stomach.

Parish's face twisted into an evil smile. "You think I'm—uuhh!" Parish's head, traveling at twenty miles per hour, smacked hard into the rocky arch of the tunnel. Dane saw a little misty spray of blood fly by, then Parish was gone, over the side of the train. Dane pressed himself flat on top of the car as the short tunnel passed by overhead. Then when they were on the other side, he stood up and hurried to the rear of the train. There, he climbed down and dropped off onto the track. He ran back down the track and through the little tunnel to look for Parish. He found him lying grotesquely twisted alongside the track, his back and neck broken. Parish was dead.

Dane went through Parish's pockets and found sixty-three dollars in cash. Then he moved the body off to the side and buried it under a pile of rocks. Later, he would come back for it to prove his claim for the reward, but for now Parish would have to stay put. Dane didn't figure Parish would mind much.

There was also a piece of paper in Parish's pocket. On the paper were three words.

Boulder Bluff, Wednesday.

Chapter 16

Morgan, Tim, and Gus were at the Claim Jumper Saloon in Boulder Bluff. Tim was at one of the other tables making an arrangement with one of the girls to go upstairs with him, Morgan was at the bar, and Gus was at a table in the back of the room, building a house of cards.

Morgan came back to the table carrying a bottle and three glasses. "Tim don't want to drink with us?"

Gus looked over at the table with Tim and the girl, then laughed, low and deep in his throat. "Tim's got other things on his mind," he said.

Morgan poured the whiskey into two glasses and slid one glass across the table to Gus. Gus waited until he placed the last card before he picked up the glass. When he tried to put the last card in place though, the entire construction fell down.

"Damn," he said. "I almost did it."

"See that fella down at the end of the bar there? The one all duded up in a suit?" Morgan asked.

Gus nodded.

"Seems he's a cattle buyer," Morgan said. "He'll be takin' the stage into Brimstone tomorrow, lookin' to buy a whole herd."

Gus looked at the man in interest. "That takes a lot of money, don't it?"

"Yes," Morgan said. He took a drink. "Only he ain't got none of it on him."

"Damn."

Morgan smiled. "No matter. I heard him tellin' the bartender that the money's already been sent on to the bank in Brimstone. Looks like there's goin' to be even more than we thought."

"How much is there?" Gus asked quietly, taking a drink.

"Better than twenty thousand dollars," Morgan said.

"Whooee, that's good money," Gus said. "Even better, when you figure that Al won't be here."

"Al ain't the only one won't be there," Deekus said. "If you want my thinkin', Parish won't be there, either."

"You think Calder got him, do you?"

"I'd bet on it," Morgan said.

"Well, then I reckon we won't be sharin' with Mr. Parish."

"Nope," Morgan said. "And if you want my thinkin', I don't figure to share any with Tim, either."

"How we goin' to avoid it? He's still here."

"I been thinkin' about it," Morgan said. "And I think I got it figured out." He nodded toward Tim and the bar girl he was with. "We was plannin' on goin' to Brimstone tomorrow, wasn't we?"

"Yes."

"We'll go today."

"Today?"

"Yes. Unless I miss my guess, Tim and that woman will be goin' upstairs in a little while. When they do, me an' you will just slip on out of here. We'll be in Brimstone, take care of our business, and be gone before Tim even notices we ain't around."

"He's goin' to be hoppin' mad when he finds out what we done," Gus said. "He's liable to come lookin' for us."

"What difference does it make? Calder is lookin' for us now, ain't he?" Morgan asked.

"Yeah, I guess you're right," Gus replied. "It won't make any difference whether one more man is lookin' for us or not."

"I figure on getting' out of here soon as we get the money, anyway."

"Where will you go?" Gus wanted to know.

"I don't know. Denver, perhaps. Or San Francisco. Maybe even Kansas City. How about you?"

"I'm goin' to Saint Louie," Gus said. He chuckled. "I seen me a picture of a woman on a calendar one time, holdin' up a bottle of beer. She was from Saint Louie. I believe she was the best-lookin' woman I ever seen, and I plan to go to Saint Louie and find her. And if I can't find her, then at least I can find that bottle of beer," he added, whooping with laughter.

"Hey, Morgan," Tim called, as he and the bar girl stood up at their table. "Me an' Lizzy is goin' upstairs. I'll see you fellas tomorrow for breakfast."

"Be ready to ride," Morgan said.

"I will be. Don't you worry none about that," Tim answered.

"Morgan, you think we can do it, just the two of us?" Gus asked.

"Yeah, nothin' to it," Morgan said. "Now, look. Here's the bank, here's the hotel, and here's the depot," Morgan said, using Gus's cards to diagram the job. "We'll tie the horses up out back, that way nobody will notice anything. We'll go in through the front door, take the money, and leave through the back. It'll be easy as pie."

"Yeah, it looks good," Gus said. "As long as Calder don't get wind of what we're doin'."

"Dammit, Gus, will you get off my back about Calder?" Morgan demanded, angrily brushing all the cards off onto the floor. "Didn't I tell you he won't be no problem? Soon as we get the money, we're goin' to get the hell out of here!"

"Yeah," Gus said. "*If* we get the money. What I'm afraid is, he might show up in time to keep us from doin' even that."

"Calder is a human being, not a ghost," Morgan said. "If you want to know the truth, I think the whole problem is that ever'one's so scared of him that they don't know he's no different from anybody else."

"But he is different," Gus insisted. "Anyone else would be dead by now."

"Are you changing your mind? Maybe we'd be better off just forgettin' about the money over in Brimstone. In fact, why don't we just go on down to the sheriff's office and turn ourselves in, right now?"

"I ain't changin' my mind about nothin'," Gus said. "I'm just tellin' you that we're makin' a big mistake if we don't think about Calder."

"We'll think about him later," Morgan said, standing up. "Come on, we've got to leave now if we're goin' to get over to Brimstone before the bank closes."

———

As MORGAN and Gus rode south out of town, they neither saw nor were they seen by a rider who was just approaching Boulder Bluff from the north.

———

DANE TOOK his horse to the livery stable to be fed and curried. The livery stable was also a good place to inquire about the men he was looking for.

"One of 'em's got a bad eye that sort of wonders all over the place," Dane explained to the old man who worked at the livery. "Another's got half an ear shot away, and the last one's a short runty little fella."

"Well, yes, sir," the old man at the livery answered. "Them three rode in a couple days ago. But two of 'em's gone, now. They rode out of here no more'n an hour ago."

"Only two of them rode away, you say? There's one still in town?"

"Yep." The stableman pointed to a star-faced gelding. "That would be the mount of the one that's still here," he said. "He's the one with only half an ear."

"That's Tim Tyrell," Dane said. "Mister, I'm much obliged to you."

———

OVER IN THE Claim Jumper Saloon, the bartender picked up a couple of whiskey glasses and saw that there was nearly an inch of whiskey left in each of them. He shrugged his shoulders, then removed the cap from the whiskey bottle and poured the liquor back into its original container.

"Whiskey," a low, quiet voice said.

When the bartender looked up, he saw a big man with a misshapen nose, and cold, blue eyes. His manner was confident and assured, and he wore his gun slung low and kicked out.

"I said, whiskey," Dane said again.

"Oh, uh, yes. Yes, of course," the bartender

replied nervously. He started to pour whiskey from the bottle he had just put the leftovers into.

"I prefer a new bottle," Dane said.

"Oh. All right." The bartender picked up a new bottle, but he was so nervous that as he started to pour, his hands began shaking badly.

"Here, let me do it," Dane offered, taking the bottle from him. Dane poured a glass and set the bottle back down. "My name is Dane Calder," he said. "And I'm looking for someone who may be in here."

Someone close by heard Dane give his name, and he gave it to another, who passed it on to another still, until soon the name was on everyone's lips, for there was no one here who hadn't heard of *the* bounty hunter.

"Who, uh—" the bartender started to say, then he had to clear his throat and lick his lips before he could finish his question. "Who are you looking for?"

"His name is Tim Tyrell," Dane answered. "You may not recognize his name, but you would remember him if you saw him. Half of one ear has been shot away." Dane put his hand to his earlobe.

The bartender's eyes darted toward the head of the stairs at the room where Tim had gone with the woman.

"I see," Dane said, smiling easily. "He's upstairs."

"I didn't say that," the bartender insisted.

"You didn't have to," Dane replied.

"What do you want with him?"

"Mister, I believe you already know that," Dane answered. "I intend to take him in…or kill him."

Dane said the words quietly, but within seconds it had spread all over the bar, just as his name had earlier. Conversations, poker games, and just plain drinking stopped as the patrons all looked at the bounty hunter.

"What did you say, mister?" someone asked.

Dane looked toward the speaker and saw that it was an older man who had just come in through the batwing doors. He was wearing a badge.

"You must be the sheriff."

"I am. And I'll not allow any cold-blooded killing in my town," the sheriff added nervously.

"I appreciate that, Sheriff," Dane said. "I do not intend to kill him in cold blood. I will first challenge him and give him an opportunity to give himself up. But if he goes for his guns, I'll have no choice but to defend myself."

"Fair enough," the sheriff said, clearing his throat. He looked around at the others in the barroom. "You heard the gent, fellas. He's promised me that it'll be a fair fight. I aim to let him brace the man he's after, and I'll make no move to the contrary unless, in my opinion, it ain't all on the up 'n up."

"That's the way it ought to be done, Sheriff," one of the others agreed.

Dane nodded and turned back to the bar.

The piano player, who had stopped for the

discourse, now began to play again. However, all eyes were on the top of the stairs, and all conversation directed toward the upcoming gunfight. Within a moment the piano had stopped again, and everyone in the saloon waited.

The waiting grew more strained, and the conversation soon petered out. Now there was absolute silence, and when someone coughed nervously, everyone turned to look at him accusingly. The clock on the wall ticked loudly as the pendulum swung back and forth. Involuntarily, perhaps a dozen or so men looked at the clock as if it were very important to fix the time in their minds, the better for the telling of their stories later.

Whiskey glasses were refilled as quietly as everything else, the drinkers merely walking over to the bar and holding their glasses out silently.

More people drifted into the saloon, but they were met at the door, and a whispered exchange told them what was going on. Most who wandered in stayed, drawing on their beer or whiskey as silently as the others.

They all waited.

The tension grew almost unbearable. From the room at the top of the stairs, came the sounds that told every man in the saloon what was going on up there. Normally, those sounds would have elicited peals of embarrassed laughter, but now they brought only silence.

The man upstairs said something, his voice a low rumble, and it was answered by a peal of laughter from the woman. There was the sound of footfalls as boots struck the floor, and the man and woman came out of the room, laughing and talking to each other. They had started down the stairs before they noticed the deathly silence and the eyes staring up at them.

"Honey, what is this? What's going on?" the woman asked, her voice strained with fright.

"Better get back out of the way," Tim ordered.

"Hello, Tim," Dane said almost pleasantly, stepping away from the bar and looking up toward him.

Inexplicably, Tim grinned. "Well, so we meet again, do we, Mr. Calder?" Tim began glancing quickly around the room.

"If you're looking for the other two, they aren't here to help you," Dane said.

"Did you get them already?"

"No. They've gone on. I'm afraid they left you behind, Tim."

"Why, them dirty bastards," Tim said. Then he smiled. "Well, you know what they say, there's no honor among thieves."

"Tim, this man is the sheriff here," Dane said, pointing to the man with the badge. "If you'll give yourself up, I'll turn you over to him. You're worth just as much to me alive as you are dead, and to be honest, you're the only one of the whole bunch I would rather take in alive."

"Well, now, I appreciate that, Calder, I really do," Tim said. He smiled again. "But you might remember that the last time we met, I was waitin' to get myself hung. Now, if I surrender to this sheriff, what's he goin' to do but send me back to Thunder Ridge where a gallows is waiting? I'm sorry, Calder. I can't give myself up."

"Don't do it, Tim."

Even as Dane was warning him, however, Tim's hand was dipping to his holster, clawing for his gun. Dane had his own gun out so fast that his hand was a blur. His shot hit Tim in the chest. Tim slammed back against the wall, then he tumbled forward and slid down the stairs headfirst. Dane hurried over to him and turned him over. Tim opened his eyes and looked up at him. His eyes were clouded with pain.

"Damn," Tim said. "Damn, if I had known it was going to hurt this much, I would've gone back to let 'em hang me."

"The rope would hurt more," Dane said.

"Yeah, yeah, I guess you're right," Tim said. His words were coming hard now. "So Morgan and Gus left me, did they?"

"Yes."

"Brimstone."

"What?"

"You'll find them in Brimstone," Tim gasped.

"Thanks."

"Serves the bastards right," Tim said, his voice just a whisper now. "Damn, this hurts."

Those were his last words.

Chapter 17

When Dane got back to the livery, the old stableman who had given him the information on the three men when he arrived was standing in the door.

"Did you feed my horse?" Dane asked.

"Yep. Rubbed him down too."

"That's good," Dane said. "He's going to need it." He took his saddle down from the top of the stall and threw it onto his horse's back.

"I heard shootin' over in the saloon," the stableman said. "You?"

"Yes."

"Figured it was. I reckon you're goin' after the other two now."

Dane led his horse over to the watering trough and the animal began to drink.

"They're in Brimstone."

"That's about ten miles south of here."

When the horse had drunk its fill, it raised its

head up from the trough, water still dripping from his lips. Dane swung up into the saddle.

"Just about as far as a horse can go at a gallop," he said. He reached down and patted the neck of his mount.

"You're going to run him all the way?"

"Got to," Dane said. "I'm not lettin' those bastards get away from me this time."

Dane let the horse trot until there were out of town, then he slapped his legs against the animal's sides and it broke into a gallop. Dane settled back into the saddle, matching the horse's rhythm with an easy, rocking motion. He could feel the wind in his face and hear drumming of hooves as the horse kicked up little spurts of dust behind him. He let himself flow into the horse so that for the duration of the run, it was as if they were sharing the same muscle structure and bloodstream.

As he rode, Dane thought of the task before him. This was the day of reckoning for Morgan Cottrell. Of that, he had no doubts.

———

EVEN AS DANE galloped toward the town, chaos was unfolding at the Bank of Brimstone. Morgan Cottrell and Gus McMein, who were no strangers to ruthless tactics, had burst into the bank. The bank president, Warren Shepherd, and a lone customer were cornered against the wall, hands raised in terror. Delbert Maroon, the teller, was frantically stuffing bundles of cash into a burlap sack provided by Morgan.

"Hurry up, hurry up, put all the money in the sack," Morgan ordered, his voice echoing through the high-ceilinged room.

"Yes, sir, I'm trying, sir. Please, don't shoot," Delbert pleaded, his hands shaking visibly as he gripped the sack.

Gus, stationed at the entrance, kept a sharp eye on the street. "There's a woman comin' this way."

Before Morgan could respond, the front door swung open. A middle-aged woman, elegantly dressed and composed, entered the bank. "Warren, I came to—" Her words cut off as her eyes registered what was happening before her.

"Miranda, leave now!" Warren cried out, but it was too late.

Morgan's grin widened. "What good timin'." He sneered, signaling Gus with a nod.

As Gus grabbed Miranda's arm, pulling her into the fray, Warren's face drained of color. "Please, let her go. Take me instead!"

Ignoring Warren's plea, Morgan shoved him back against the wall. "She ain't got no choice, mister. She's here whether she likes it or not."

Miranda's fear was evident, but she composed herself quickly, her eyes darting around, assessing the situation. As Gus tried to tie her hands, she stomped on his foot and elbowed him in the ribs, causing him to grunt in pain.

Morgan laughed cruelly. "Feisty little lady, ain't ya?"

Outside, a gentleman was approaching the bank. He saw what was happening and turned to run. "The bank's being robbed! Everybody arm yourselves," he yelled.

Morgan peeked through the dusty window, noting how townspeople were heading toward the bank carrying guns or whatever else they could pick up to use as a weapon. "Looks like these folks is darin' us to kill 'em," he said.

"They're surroundin' us!" Gus exclaimed, peeking through a side window.

Warren seized the moment of distraction. "You won't get far with all these people outside. Let my wife go, and maybe they'll let you pass."

Morgan considered this briefly, then shook his head with a smirk. "Nope, that ain't goin' to happen. She's our ticket out of here. We're going out the front door, and we're goin' in style. We're getting' us a train."

Miranda, now somewhat composed, spoke up. "If you think these people will let you walk out with me, you're more foolish than you look. This town sticks together."

Morgan's eyes narrowed. "That so? Well then, let's see how far that goes." He turned to Miranda. "Pick up that bag, honey. You're leadin' the parade."

Miranda lifted the heavy sack, her resolve hardening. "You'll pay for this, Bud. Maybe not today, but soon."

Morgan's only response was a cold mirthless laugh as he ushered her toward the door, his gun pressed firmly against her back. The townspeople's voices grew louder, with anger and determination swelling just outside.

———

DANE HAD BEEN RIDING HARD, and it had taken him just slightly over half an hour to bridge the distance between Boulder Bluff and Brimstone. As he entered Brimstone, his horse slowed from a trot to a cooling walk amid the chaos of the town center. A crowd was milling about in the street, their voices sounding of anger and confusion as their attention was divided between the bank and the railroad depot.

Calder dismounted with practiced ease, his body aching, from the result of his ride. He tied his sweating horse to the hitching rail in front of the sheriff's office and used his hat to swipe at the trail dust coating his clothes. Stepping inside, he was greeted by the sight of the deputy, a young man barely in his twenties, gazing out the window, his attention fixed on the street.

The deputy turned as the door creaked open, his eyes narrowing slightly as he appraised Dane. "Somethin' I can do for you, mister?" he asked, his tone casual yet cautious as he sipped his coffee.

"I need to see the sheriff," Dane stated, his voice in a state of urgency.

"He ain't here," the deputy replied, nodding toward the chaos outside. "Case you didn't notice when you rode in here, we got us a situation goin'."

"You just had your bank robbed," Dane said, his eyes not leaving the deputy's.

The deputy paused, the cup halting midway to his lips, then he set it down with a clink. "Yeah, it was," he confirmed, his suspicion evident. "How'd you know?"

"Call it a lucky guess," Dane responded coolly. "Now, where's the sheriff?"

"He's out there." The deputy pointed toward a tall, skinny figure standing by the hitching rail in front of the general store. "He's dealing with all this mess. Whatever you need, it better be important."

"Look at my horse, Deputy," Dane said, gesturing toward the exhausted animal. "Would I ride him half to death if it wasn't?"

The deputy followed his gaze and nodded. "All right then," he said. "You better catch him quick."

Dane nodded and stepped back into the sunbaked street, his eyes scanning the crowd. He made his way toward the sheriff, each step purposeful, aware that every moment counted. Behind him, the deputy watched, his earlier indifference replaced by a realization that this stranger might be able to quell this situation.

As Dane approached the sheriff, the sound of agitated voices grew louder, a reflection of the panic that was going through the crowd. He needed to act, and fast, if he was to stop Morgan Cottrell from causing more chaos and killing.

———

DANE PICKED his way through the crowd until he reached the sheriff. The sheriff was surrounded by a half-dozen townspeople.

"You've got to do something, Sheriff," a portly, well-dressed man was saying. "That's my wife they have in there."

"Well now, Warren, you just tell me what it is you want me to do, and I'll be glad to do it," the sheriff answered with a long-suffering sigh.

"I want you to go into that depot and get my wife. That's what I want," the banker said.

From the depot, a new round of shouts erupted, followed by the sound of a single gunshot, silencing the murmurs in the crowd. A tense quiet fell over the street.

"Get off the street!" the sheriff shouted, waving the people aside. "Ever'one, get off the street!"

Men and women dashed in between the buildings and dived for cover behind porches and watering troughs. Several ran inside. The sheriff stepped up onto the front porch of the general store. All were staring toward the railroad depot, which was located at the far end of the street.

"That was real smart of you, Sheriff!" a voice shouted down from the depot. "You tell ever'body to just keep their distance, and no one else will get hurt."

"What is it you want?" the sheriff called.

"I'm sendin' somebody down to talk to you," the voice said. "He'll tell you all about it."

The door to the depot opened and someone came out onto the platform. He hesitated for a moment, then put his hands up.

"Sheriff, there's somebody comin'!" someone shouted.

"Don't shoot!" the man with the raised hands called from the depot platform. "Don't nobody shoot! It's me, Jacob Groves!"

"It's Jacob Groves," someone shouted, as if Jacob hadn't already identified himself.

"It's me, the telegrapher!" Jacob yelled again, moving slowly, cautiously down the street, his hands stuck high in the air.

"Come ahead, Jacob," the sheriff called.

"Don't shoot!" Jacob called again.

"Dammit, Jacob, we ain't gonna shoot," the sheriff said. "Come ahead."

Walking slowly, and obviously very frightened, Jacob moved down the street toward the middle of town, all the while keeping his hands high in the air.

"Put your hands down, Jacob, you ain't our prisoner," the sheriff said calmly, as Jacob reached the front porch of the general store.

"Thank goodness," Jacob said, lowering his arms. "Thank goodness, I'm out of there."

"How many are in there?" Dane asked.

The sheriff looked around then, noticing Dane for the first time.

"Who the devil are you?" the sheriff asked.

"The name is Calder. Dane Calder. I've been trailing Morgan Cottrell and Gus McMein for some time now. Unless I miss my guess, I've caught up with 'em."

"I don't know if that's who we have in there or not," the sheriff said. "But whoever it is, it ain't your problem now. It's mine."

"Wrong, Sheriff," Dane replied coldly. "I've chased them this far. I'm not about to walk away now."

"Dane Calder, you say? Yes, I've heard of you, Mr. Calder. You're the one they call *the* bounty hunter."

Dane didn't answer.

"Well, Mr. Bounty Hunter, we ain't even sure that's who we got in there. So why don't you just stay back out of the way and let me take care of my business?"

"That's who's in there, all right, Sheriff," Jacob said. "Morgan Cottrell and Gus McMein. And they done seen you too, mister," he added, looking at Dane. "They want you to come in there. They said they want to talk to you."

"That's all they want? To talk to Dane Calder?" the sheriff asked.

"That and a train," Jacob replied.

"A train?"

"Yes, Sheriff, they want you to stop the next train

to come through here, disconnect all the cars but one, then they're goin' to get on it...with Mrs. Shepherd," Jacob said, looking at Warren.

"Oh no! They're taking my wife with them?"

"And Mr. Calder," Jacob added. "They said if we do ever'thing they ask, they'll set Mrs. Shepherd down from the train, safe and sound, about five miles from here."

"Do it, man, do it!" Warren Shepherd demanded.

"What about Calder?"

Jacob hesitated, his gaze fixed on the ground, afraid to answer.

"What did they say about Calder?" the sheriff said, pressing for details.

Jacob swallowed hard before answering. "They, uh, said they had other plans for him."

Dane, who had been quietly observing, chuckled darkly. "I'll just bet they do," Dane said, stepping down from the porch. Without waiting for a response, he began walking toward the depot.

"Here!" the sheriff called after him. "Calder, where do you think you're going?"

"I'm goin' to talk to them," Calder called back over his shoulder. "That's what they want, isn't it?"

"I can't let you do that," the sheriff protested. "You know what they plan to do with you."

"Let him go!" Warren demanded. "He's a bounty hunter—he's used to dealing with these kinds of people."

"No," the sheriff insisted. "Calder, you come back here. I will not let you go down there."

"Sheriff, shoot me in the back or else just shut up," Calder replied, his tone resolute. The crowd watched in silence as he continued his approach to the depot.

As Dane stepped up onto the platform and entered the building, he was greeted by a stark contrast. The bright sunshine gave way to dim, shadowed interiors. Inside, Morgan and Gus were waiting, their expressions a mix of amusement and surprise.

"Well now," Morgan said, a smirk spreading across his face. "Lookee here who we got, Gus. He just come walkin' right in here, as pretty as you please."

Standing in the middle of the room, Morgan held a pistol to Mrs. Shepherd's temple. Gus was by the window, keeping an eye on the street outside.

"I thought you was supposed to be a smart man, Calder," Gus taunted from his post. "But you was dumb to come in here like this."

"Isn't that what you asked me to do?" Dane countered calmly.

Gus laughed. "Did you hear that, Morgan? He come in here because we *asked* him to. If we'd know'd how easy it was gonna be, we could'a asked him a long time ago to just come walkin' up to us so we could shoot him."

"You may as well let the woman go," Dane said,

his gaze never leaving Morgan. "She won't do you any good."

"Are you kiddin'?" Morgan replied mockingly. "She's our ticket out of here."

"No," Dane said, "she's not."

Morgan blinked, taken aback by Dane's comment. "What do you mean, she's not?"

"I mean, I'm not letting you leave with or without her," Dane stated firmly.

Morgan laughed, though his eyes showed a hint of unease. "You must be crazy," he said. "Make one little move and I'll kill this woman. You don't understand, I don't give a damn whether I kill this woman or not."

"No, *you* don't understand," Dane shot back. "*I* don't give a damn whether you kill her or not. I'm goin' to kill you."

Morgan's expression shifted from confidence to fear as Dane's hand twitched toward his gun. Caught in a dilemma, Morgan hesitated—a fatal mistake. By the time he decided to defend himself, it was too late. Dane's gun was already drawn, the hammer falling on the primer.

The depot became deathly quiet. Gus, witnessing the fall of Morgan, had only moments to react. He had thought that the threat against Mrs. Shepherd would stall Dane, but that evaporated as he saw the fatal wound marking the end of his partner.

With a panic-driven shout, Gus whipped around, his gun swinging away from the window where he had been keeping watch. His movements were desperate and swift. He aimed shakily at Dane, the only thought in his mind to shoot before he could be shot.

However, Gus's reaction, swift as it was, couldn't match Dane's cold precision. Dane had already anticipated Gus's desperation. As Gus's finger tightened on the trigger, his shot rang out—a thunderous sound that echoed through the empty depot.

Gus's shot went wild, his bullet embedding itself harmlessly into the wooded floor. Almost simultaneously, Dane's bullet found its mark with deadly accuracy. The impact sent Gus staggering backward, a stunned look on his face as he processed the searing pain in his chest.

He crumpled to the floor with a .44 slug in his heart. The gun slipped from his limp hand, clattering against the wood.

Dane stood over the two outlaws, his breathing steady despite what had just happened. The depot was suddenly very quiet, the echoes of gunshots quickly fading. He turned his attention to Mrs. Shepherd, who stood frozen, her eyes wide with terror and relief.

"It's over," Dane said softly. He holstered his gun and carefully approached her, his movements deliberate, meant to reassure. "Let's get you back to your husband."

————

As Mrs. Shepherd and Dane emerged from the shadowy confines of the depot into the bright afternoon sun, the tension was broken. A shout rose from the crowd, a mixture of relief and disbelief.

"Someone's comin'!"

"Hold your fire! It's the woman!"

"And Calder! He got her out of there!"

The onlookers, who had been a mix of nervous anxiousness just moments before, began moving toward the railroad station. Warren Shepherd broke his way through the crowd.

"Miranda! Miranda, are you all right?" Warren called out, his voice cracking with emotion.

Miranda broke into a run with a surprising burst of energy for someone who had just been through such an ordeal. She met Warren halfway, and he took her into his arms. The crowd surged forward, surrounding them as they realized the immediate danger had passed.

"Where are Cottrell and McMein?" the sheriff asked, stepping forward as Dane approached.

"Inside," Dane said flatly. "I killed them both."

"You were in there and shot it out with them while they were holding this woman hostage? What's wrong with you? Don't you have a lick of concern about anyone's life? Just who do you think you are?" the sheriff demanded, his voice rising in a mix of anger and disbelief.

Miranda, her spirit unbroken despite what she had just been through, stepped forward, her gaze fierce. "Sheriff," she said, placing a calming hand on his arm, "listen to yourself. What are you talking about? Why are you shouting at him? Don't you realize that this man saved my life?"

"Yes, but he—he—" the sheriff sputtered, his anger faltering under her steady gaze.

"He what?" Miranda pressed, her voice strong and clear. She turned to the gathered crowd, her posture commanding their attention. "This man," she gestured toward Dane, "acted with courage when we needed it most. He deserves more than our thanks."

The sheriff looked from Miranda to Dane, and the tension slowly left his shoulders as he sighed. "I guess I do owe you my thanks," he admitted. He swept his hand toward the crowd. "In fact, we all owe you our thanks."

"Keep your thanks, Sheriff," Dane replied gruffly. "There are two corpses lying on the floor of the depot in there, and there's paper out on both of 'em. All I want from you is the reward that is my due for sending their miserable souls to hell."

As the crowd murmured, Miranda looked at Dane with a mixture of admiration and sorrow. "Sometimes, justice comes at a harsh price," she said, her voice carrying softly to those nearby.

Dane met her gaze, a hint of weariness in his eyes. "It does, ma'am, but it's a price I'm willing to pay."

A Look At:

Hidden Hero

SECRETS, LOVE, AND GUNFIGHTS COLLIDE IN THE OLD WEST.

Smith is just a barroom piano player in Casper, Wyoming, with a secret—the kind of secret that gets men killed.

When young Eliza Whitlock arrives in town, she quickly falls in love with Smith. But an ambitious man working for her father, a stagecoach tycoon, has other plans for Eliza —and for the town of Casper. His scheme is simple: destroy the local stage line, take control of the town, and force Eliza into a marriage, earning her father's approval in the process.

As bullets fly and the townsmen take sides in the fight for the lucrative stage route in and out of Casper, Smith digs his heels in to help the town. Too bad a gunslick discovers his secret in the process and decides to give the piano man a one-way ticket to hell.

Will hidden hero Smith survive the deadly schemes and save Casper? Dive into this gripping Western tale and find out!

AVAILABLE OCTOBER 2024

About the Author

Robert Vaughan sold his first book when he was nineteen. That was several years and nearly five-hundred books ago. Since then, he has written the novelization for the mini-series Andersonville, as well as wrote, produced, and appeared in the History Channel documentary Vietnam Homecoming.

Vaughan's books have hit the *NYT* bestseller list seven times. He has won the Spur Award, the Porgie Award in Best Paperback Original, the Western Fictioneers Lifetime Achievement Award, the Read-west President's Award for Excellence in Western Fiction, and is a member of the American Writers Hall of Fame and a Pulitzer Prize nominee.

He is also a retired army officer, helicopter pilot with three tours in Vietnam, who has received the Distinguished Flying Cross, the Purple Heart, The Bronze Star with three oak leaf clusters, the Air Medal for valor with 35 oak leaf clusters, the Army Commendation Medal, the Meritorious Service Medal, and the Vietnamese Cross of Gallantry.

Made in United States
Troutdale, OR
02/26/2025